The lure of the sea! What happens when petite, young first-timers sail the waters in the company of big, burly seamen? They gain experience!

Angles and Dangles is the story of Rex Dongiovanni, a big, muscled seaman third class in the US Navy assigned to a submarine where "140 men go down, and 70 couples surface."

In **The Able Seaman**, Paxton Smalls finds his best asset is behind him, and what's in front is of little consequence. He shares his bounty with the merchant marines aboard his tramp vessel as they head towards a tight passage through the Straits of Magellan.

Panama Heat tells the romantic story of young Quentin Fournier, who loves to give big, strong men what they crave. On the lam, he catches a ship bound for the construction site of the Panama Canal. He falls for Dale Clark, a man with a big problem; Quentin finds that his wide passageway rivals the Canal!

BOBBING BUOYS AND SALTY SEAMEN

Gay Erotic Seafaring Tales

PETER SCHUTES
ADAM MAXWELL BIGGLESWORTH

CONTENTS

Come; let us squeeze hands all around; nay, let us all squeeze ourselves into each other; let us squeeze ourselves universally into the very milk and sperm of human kindness. Would that I could keep squeezing that sperm for ever!

—Ishmael, Moby Dick

❧ I ❧
ANGLES AND DANGLES
BY ADAM MAXWELL
BIGGLESWORTH

ANGLES AND DANGLES

BY ADAM MAXWELL BIGGLESWORTH

My name is Rex Dongiovanni, and my rank is Seaman Third Class. My first assignment was to the submarine Guadalupe Vallejo under way to the Philippines out of Mare Island. Before I launch into my story, let me tell you a little bit about life on a submarine. You've probably heard the old saying, "On a submarine, 140 men go down, and 70 couples surface." It's not just a saying, as I found out. This happens partly because they have an eighteen-hour rotation, which means you're eighteen hours on and twelve hours off for recreation and sleep. They put you "three to a rack" - it means that you sleep two to a bunk, with nothing but a little curtain between you. You sleep in staggered shifts. Every six hours, someone wakes up, and someone else takes their place. So you're trying to get to sleep next to one guy, and then six hours later, another one takes his place. It's like the dating game. You're supposed to sleep for the whole eight hours, but instead, you wake up with a boner, and, well, stuff happens.

Me, I won't lie; when God was handing out dicks, I musta been first in line because I had one that's more than twice as big as the next biggest guy on the submarine. It's impossible to hide in the white polyester sailor pants. There's not a man on the ship who doesn't know about my huge, fat dong. They call me "Dong-Giovanni." I try to pretend it doesn't hurt, but it does because I had absolutely no luck with the ladies. They all heard about my "big problem." High school locker room showers reveal all, and guys gossip just as much as women. So they all tried to get me in the sack. As soon as they saw what I was packing, they chickened out. Every last one. I was a virgin when I enlisted in the Navy. The guys didn't know that. They figured a big swinging dong was a ticket to endless sex. But mine was a barrier. Until I met Harvey Pettit. But I'll get to that.

There are some other little sayings that tell you about how we deal with sex on a sub. "It's not gay if you're under way." The other is, "If you see the curtain rocking, keep on walking." Stuff like that tells you that when men are trapped together, you just throw away all the hang-ups from the surface and adapt.

So that's what happened. I was sleeping when this kid half my size crawled into his bunk, bumping me and waking me up. I pulled back the curtain to yell at him, and I saw Harvey Pettit, with his flossy white hair and deep blue eyes, and something snapped. I was hooked. His eyes went straight to my crotch. He knew what everyone was saying. But he didn't look scared at all.

I was nineteen, and you know what that means. I got a boner in seconds flat. It rose up off my leg and lifted my blanket. Harvey didn't hesitate one bit. He just pulled off the blanket, yanked down my shorts, and put his little mouth on the head of my big cock. A couple of ladies had tried that and gave up. Harvey was different. He had crazy skills. He unhitched his jaw like a snake and put the whole head in his mouth. It was the first time I'd ever gotten this far.

I said, "Holy shit, dude, how did you do that?"

He couldn't answer, but he just kept pushing forward until some of the shaft slipped past his lips. I felt the head hit his tonsils, and keep going. A lump in his throat told me I was going deep. He got about halfway down my shaft before he ran out of air and came up. His eyes had tears in them.

He said, "I want you to fuck me."

I'd only ever tried it with one dude, and he was just as scared as the girls. He wanted to fuck me instead, and I wouldn't let him. I was strictly a fucker and never a fuckee. That was how I framed it in my mind. I hadn't really ever proven it, though. Until Harvey.

The beautiful kid rolled so he was facing away from me and pulled down his shorts. His butt was round and soft. I rubbed it, thinking how he was going to back down when I tried to put it in. He had hand cream, which he rubbed all up in his hole. I saw his fingers disappear into the hole, then he spread them, so I could almost see into his ass. He had all four fingers in there, then he slipped his thumb in. He pushed, and his whole hand disappeared up there. I thought I was gonna come just watching him.

Harvey made a fist and pulled out, making his hole hang open. He did this a dozen times or so, then reached behind and grabbed the top of my dick, pulling it off my chest. He angled it just right so the head pressed against his hole. He wriggled towards me, and the head just popped right in.

I heard Harvey whisper. "Shit, that's big."

He paused there, and I thought he was going to quit, but he didn't. He scooted onto my mattress, pushing more of my dick inside. Then I felt the end of his ass. I was maybe halfway in and couldn't really go any further, or so I thought. Harvey lifted his leg and twisted, and with a loud pop, I felt my cock go into another hole. I realized it was going into his guts. It felt like I'd torn a hole in him.

I was worried. "Are you okay?"

Harvey said, "Yeah, dude, it's cool. Feels so fucking good."

He pushed himself closer to me until I could feel my pubes tickling his butt cheeks.

"You're so fucking huge. Christ!"

He wriggled and pushed some more until his cheeks hit my hip bones. He spread his cheeks and took the last inch of my dick. I was all the way inside now. It felt amazing. My hips took over, pumping and humping him from the side. I was too excited. I felt my balls pull up tight.

"Harvey, I'm gonna come."

He didn't say shit. He squeezed my dick with his ass muscles like he was milking a cow. I felt faint like I might pass out. My dick was swollen to its maximum size, and it needed a lot of blood to get there. Then I snapped out of it when the orgasm came.

I'd jacked off plenty; had to. But coming inside another man was so different. It wasn't just because every inch of my long, long meat was getting stimulated, unlike a hand. It was also this powerful feeling of dominating the kid. He was submitting to me, letting me invade him. So when I came, it was mind-blowing. I was putting my come up inside another man.

"Oh fuck!" I tried to keep quiet, but it was hard. I heard someone shush me from a nearby bunk. I bit down hard on my lip and gushed a flood of come. I was holding Harvey by the waist. I felt something splatter on my fingers. He'd come without touching himself.

He leaned his head back and pulled me close. We kissed. I was still buried up inside him. I was still hard. The kiss was too exciting. I needed to come again. I didn't have to say it. The electricity between us told him everything. He moved his hips, stroking my cock with his guts. He put a hand on his belly, and I felt it. I was poking his belly button. We kissed and kissed. I didn't want to let him go. He didn't want it, either. He put a hand around my neck and rode my cock like a pony. I wanted so badly to fuck him from the top, but the bunk was like a coffin. There was no way a man could lie on top of another. But Harvey's little ass just kept stroking my dick as he pulled and pushed. He took longer strokes, wriggling like a snake, until my head popped out of that hole again, making another sound. Then pop! Back in. He kept at it until it sounded like someone clapping.

"Keep it down!" Some angry seaman was not enjoying the sound. I didn't care. Each time I popped in or out, my cock head throbbed. It was softer and wetter than my hand, but it reminded me of jacking off when I rubbed up and down my head, except it was Harvey doing all the work.

"Knock it off!" Another angry seaman must have woken up. Harvey pushed away, so half my cock was exposed to the air. He stopped pushing deep, and instead, he popped my dick in and out of his asshole. Each time he pulled away, I saw it hang open, with gray pussy lips, bright red inside. That was too much. I never realized my cock could do that - stretch a boy's hole so wide it didn't close up. Seeing it and thinking about it put me in that zone where it feels like a sneeze coming on, but it never quite comes. Over and over, I felt an orgasm try to escape, but it receded, like an ocean wave crashing on shore and then drawing back.

"Ungh!" Harvey must have come again. I put my hand on his penis for the first time. His crotch was wet, but it felt like there was no dick. I moved my hand around and found a little nipple-like protrusion. He held my wrist and put my hand on his ass.

"You don't need to touch it," he whispered.

But that made me want to. I put my hand back and rubbed it, feeling the tiny penis roll across my palm. I couldn't see it, but I was sure it was the smallest one I'd ever encountered. I saw small guys in the showers, but they had more than Harvey.

His little pecker hardened up, but it was still as small as a pinky toe on a tiny foot. It turned me on. It made me feel even more powerful. I think power is the ultimate turn-on for me because that was the thought that put me over the edge.

Squeezing that tiny penis, I pushed forward with one last pop until I was buried inside him, then I let loose another torrent of come. I felt him come in my hand. I kept rubbing, but he pulled my hand away.

"It's too sensitive."

I felt a little bit of envy. Harvey had this itty bitty prick that was so sensitive he had to push me away. What would it feel like to have almost nothing between my legs? Thinking about it got me hard again. Harvey must have felt me swelling up.

"I need to sleep now." He pulled away, then rolled over so I could see him from the front. His tiny soft penis sat on almost invisible balls, like one of those Italian statues.

I whispered. "Your cock is fucking beautiful."

He blushed. "It's too small."

"It's perfect." It was. I loved how powerful I felt when I saw it. He was everything I wasn't. Short, blond, skinny, and no dick. I was tall, black-haired, brown-eyed, muscular, with a dick three times as thick and long as an average guy. A six-pack of dick. Harvey was like a hundredth my size. It was so fucking hot.

He stared at my throbbing cock, marveling.

"I'm not going to sleep thinking about it," he said.

"Me neither."

Harvey fell asleep, but I had to jerk off to get rid of my hardon. My hand kept banging against the curtain. I had to lie on my side because my dick was too long. I would have pounded the ceiling, jerking off on my back. I came all over the curtain. I wasn't the first. It was full of come stains. I drifted off to be rudely awoken two hours later. Harvey snored away; six hours to go.

Harvey was not on his first voyage, and he knew the ropes. He got us permanently assigned to the same bunk. I slept six hours, waking up when Harvey swapped out with another officer. I had my morning sex, and he had his evening sex. It was morning after morning of fucking (night after night for Harvey). We never saw sunlight, which made us kind of crazy. The trip across the Pacific was endless. It was the longest journey a sub usually made, and there were no ports between San Francisco and Manila. Other sailors paired up with each other. You heard the curtains knocking all night, really. Or it might have been all day. My internal clock was busted.

I was a third-class seaman, like I said. It's the lowest rank. I was in training. Harvey was a seaman second class, so he got more time off, and he got to eat dessert, smoke cigarettes, and watch movies. That was all forbidden to a third-class seaman. Every waking hour was meant to be devoted to learning all about the sub and its inner workings. Still, in the one hour of free time, Harvey showed me a utility closet that the guys called "the jack shack." It was a place for guys who liked to jerk off standing up. It was also a good place for a quickie. These days, it takes me an hour to come, but at nineteen, I needed less than ten minutes.

When he showed it to me, I fucked the shit out of Harvey in that closet. He pulled the door closed, facing me, and dropped his pants. I raced to get my dick out before it got trapped down the leg of my pants. It popped out, hitting Harvey on the chin. He laughed.

"Sorry, brother."

Harvey said, "You can hit me anytime, anywhere, with that fucking beautiful cock."

In high school, I thought my dick was big and ugly, but Harvey had convinced me otherwise.

I couldn't wait to do it face-to-face. I squatted down and lifted Harvey up until his ass lined up with my cock head, and then I impaled him. He leaned against the wall of the closet while I held him mid-air, fucking him. I leaned forward until our lips met, eyes open, staring into each other's souls. Gravity was kind; I buried myself to the root. Harvey didn't have to spread his cheeks; my pelvis did it for him. For the first time, I saw the lump moving up and down his belly. I saw my cock in relief, and it was glorious. Harvey looked down and smiled.

"Cool." He pressed his hands against his belly button until I felt the squeeze. Then something extraordinary happened.

Harvey's eyes fluttered. "Oh shit, what is that?" He looked surprised, and it didn't take long before I knew what he was asking. His guts were contracting, squeezing my cock involuntarily. He bucked and thrashed, eyes wild and wide.

"Oh, Jesus! Oh, holy Christ! Oh fuck!" Harvey was in ecstasy, and so was I. Having every inch of your cock inside a man is bliss, but when it's cramping and flexing all around you, it's like nothing on this earth. It was freaky alien sex.

Harvey said, "Oh god, I'm coming like a bitch." Emphasizing his words, his little tiny cock spurted on my belly and chest. I held his bottom, lifting and dropping him over and over as he orgasmed on the inside. After another minute, he came again. The squeezing and clamping got faster. I felt waves traveling up and down my cock. I kissed him, and in another minute, he and I came in unison. As his cock spurted his semen until it ran down into my pubes, I filled his colon with my manly come.

At last, the waves of pressure subsided, and Harvey stopped jerking and thrashing. I touched his beautiful right nipple, and he jumped, milking out the last load of come from the tip of my cock. When I pulled out, gravity brought the whole messy load with it. The utility closet floor was sticky with the come of 140 sailors. None of them could possibly feel as lucky as the two of us.

I was a wog, short for pollywog, which meant I hadn't crossed the Equator. Since we were bound for the Philippines, I was going to cross the line on my first voyage. There's a ceremony for wogs crossing the line. For those of you who don't know, all the folks who have crossed the Equator have all been through the line-crossing ceremony. Sailors who have crossed are called Shellbacks. The ceremony, they tell me, is pretty rough. Harvey filled me in; it all sounded pretty disgusting.

The ceremony started a week before I crossed the line. The shellbacks gave us heavy weights we used for compacting trash. We had to polish them and wear them around our necks. The day before the crossing, they gave us a hard candy they call "The Pearl." We had to carry it at all times; we couldn't eat it or lose it. But we were all naked, so we ended up sticking it up our asses. The crew set up this ice-cold plunge. They dunked us in it. Turned out that all the seamen had pissed in it. We could smell the urine.

They gave all the wogs dresses sewn out of curtains, and we performed a strip tease for the shellbacks. I was a show pony. More than one of them slapped their faces with my dick, and a couple tried to suck it. Harvey pulled the tip out of a petty officer's mouth and sucked me off in front of the whole sub. I couldn't help myself. I came in his mouth to wild cheers. Then we had to pop the candy out of our asses, and one by one, we knelt before Petty Officer Sheldice, the fattest sailor on the submarine. He was covered in whipped cream, mustard, vinegar, maple syrup, ketchup, and Tabasco. We had to use our tongues to put the stink-ass hard candy deep into his belly button, then suck and lick until it came back out. I got hard doing it, which raised a lot of eye-brows. When it was over, we got to take off the weights, shower, and get dressed. We were all shell-backs. It was one of the best things about being on the sub.

But the very best way we killed time was "Angles and Dangles." When we were in very deep waters, halfway between the surface and the bottom, they did tight angles and dips with the ship. It would roll and rise, causing plates to crash down in the galley and forcing everyone to hold on to the nearest stationary object. Some seamen greased the floors and rode cafeteria trays from stem to stern and back.

The first time they started up angles and dangles, me and Harvey were in that utility closet, fucking like jackrabbits. I reached deeper inside him than I'd ever been when we hit the wall. It nearly broke my dick in two, but it was by far the best sex yet. After that, we always planned our closet sex around that game.

A lot of guys were jealous of what me and Harvey had. They shacked up, but not like us. Usually, neither one wanted to be the girl, and it ended up just being a jack fest or maybe they took turns sucking each other off.

By the time the sub pulled into Manila, our food had nearly gone. We had only ketchup sandwiches and bouillon for breakfast, lunch, and dinner. We were starving. We had only twenty-four hours to enjoy time on the surface. Our first and only stop was a hotel with room service. We lay in the bed, fucking, ordering room service every few hours. We didn't get any sleep. I can still taste the crispy lumpia and chicken adobo. There was joy in finally laying down face to face on a soft mattress, fucking like a man and a woman, but it wasn't as good as the utility closet during angles and dangles!

I'll tell you something you might find surprising. Harvey and me, we're still together. We've both been out of the Navy for ten years, and we're still fucking every night. We bought a house in Crockett, a little town across the Straits from Mare Island, and we both work at the C&H sugar factory there. I thought my time in the Navy would be the best years of my life, but now that I'm living with Harvey, I think those years may still be ahead of us. I might take an hour to come these days, but Harvey still squirts every five minutes. We have to wash the sheets every night, it seems. We have a washer and dryer, so who cares?

II

THE ABLE SEAMAN

BY PETER SCHUTES

ABOUT THE ABLE SEAMAN

BY PETER SCHUTES

The sea calls a queer sort of folk to its shores. They board ships bound for destinations both exotic and mundane. It takes a strong man to live away from family for so long. The men without families often make their own aboard ship.

Paxton Smalls, the son of a New Orleans harlot and an unknown john, was both blessed and cursed by nature. She stole from him the gift of a normal manhood. He was nearly a woman in front. What nature took, she bestowed on his ample buttocks. Paxton had the kind of ass that sailors picture while pleasuring themselves in solitude, or even when relieving themselves with another. Society on land shamed Paxton for his shortcomings, and ridiculed him for his womanly bottom. On the sea, it was quite the opposite. With the salt spray in the air, men swooned as he passed. They wouldn't see a woman for months, but Paxton could make such men tremble and pine for the darker pleasures of man on man flesh.

Paxton was ashamed of his pitiful endowment and massive bottom when he boarded the Southern Cross. It didn't take long for him to accept his gifts for what they were, and use them the way God himself intended.

At the opposite extreme were some of the men to whom God had given too much. They suffered rejection and shame because of their massive manhood. Paxton became a vessel for their love, opening his giant bottom to let them all come inside.

SMALL PROBLEM, SAILOR'S DELIGHT

Paxton Smalls grew up in New Orleans. As a youngster, he spent a good deal of his time at the waterfront. His favorite pastime was riding the free Ferry Boat to Algiers and back. The hustle and bustle of the mercantile trade excited him. He counted and classified boats to while away the time until his mother was finished with one of his many uncles. It was on the waterfront that he fell in love. His first love was the Mississippi River, then came the Gulf of Mexico, and then every sea and ocean he could dream of. Paxton wanted to be a sailor.

Due to the nature of his mother's line of business, Paxton never met his daddy and never would. His mother told him that he was dashingly handsome but was never going to marry a girl. "It was one in a thousand he would ever put her in a family way. It just wasn't physically possible. I was just lucky, I guess." Paxton didn't know what this meant until senior year when he joined the varsity football team and had to take showers with his classmates for the first time.

Until Paxton's first locker room shower, he had no idea anything was amiss down there. He sat down to pee. He never worried about it.. But the other seniors saw his little problem right away. In a moment of horror, he discovered that he had only the tiniest fraction of what the other guys had. He ran from the showers, not even waiting for a towel, and the whole room filled with taunts and jeers. He dressed in a bathroom stall, sniffing back tears. The names rang in his ears: Teeny Peenie, Inchworm, Button Boy...the names stung.

Paxton went home to tell his mother about his deformity, but she had an uncle in the room. He had to go cry at the waterfront. He was ashamed and angry. He would never be a normal man. He drowned in shame, deciding never to discuss it with his mother. He was dying to ask how his dad got her pregnant, so he could do the same, but the shame and self-loathing were far more powerful than his curiosity. He wondered why she would choose a man who so obviously shouldn't be making babies as the one to father her child. But she had hinted it was a work-related accident and not by choice.

Paxton sought refuge in the comfort of the waterfront. Longshoremen and sailors took his mind off his shame, but the sadness returned in waves.

With his head between his knees, Paxton's tears hit the planks and tumble into the Mississippi. When he looked up, he saw a dozen sailors walking in a huddle. He was in their path. When he scrambled to his feet, he hit an oil slick. He fell hard, legs in the air. A young sailor who smelled like rum and cigars caught his arm and helped him to his feet. Paxton noticed the man wore a green carnation tattoo on his wrist. The other sailors whistled and made catcalls.

"Why they shoutin' like that?" he asked.

The sailor grinned. "You never put your legs in the air around merchant marines. Go on, jailbait. We'll just watch you to make sure you can walk okay." More whistles. Paxton was confused. In school, he only ever heard guys make that sound to flirt with pretty girls. He whirled around.

"I ain't no pretty girl!" He shouted at the whole dozen.

A sailor cried out, "Any port in a storm!" The words were mean, but his smile was genuine. They meant him no harm.

It was shaping up to be the worst day of his life. The man with the green carnation came close. He wasn't drunk - that rum smell was spice cologne. He lifted Paxton's chin, and their eyes met. Paxton saw the whole ocean in those blue eyes. He was overcome with a strange desire that drew his eyes downward to below the sailor's belt. He was sure the serpentine bulge was a trick of the fabric. Nobody was that size down there. He lifted his eyes again.

"Kid, don't let them bother you none. We just know when we see one of our own."

"A sailor?" Paxton was excited.

The man nodded. "Yeah, that's it, a sailor." He chuckled. "What's your name, kid?"

"Paxton, sir."

"Paxton, when you're ready to join the fleet of merchant marines, we'll welcome you with open arms."

The boy gave the sailor a big hug, which brought on more jeers and catcalls. Paxton didn't care. He was in love with the sea. He felt movement in the man's pants like he had a live boa in there. He stole a second glance and gasped. He touched it briefly and drew in his breath. "Is that...?"

The man lowered his head and grinned. "That's my Albatross." Paxton swooned. He had almost nothing, and this sailor had the share of three men or more. The heavily gifted sailor patted the boy's bottom and sent him on his way. The touch of his hand was gentle but firm. It made Paxton yearn to be on the open sea with these rough sailors.

Paxton was angry at God that he could play such cruel tricks with men's anatomy, giving so little to some and too much to others. He let it go. He was in the clouds and didn't know exactly why.

It was the worst day turned into the best. And not one but twelve sailors called him one of their own. He whistled as he walked home, oblivious to the heads that turned as he passed.

Paxton had another six months of school left. Impatient, he stopped into the US Merchant Marine recruiting office. Dick Williams, the officer in charge, gave the boy a great big smile.

"Paxton," he said, "you signing up?"

Paxton had seen Dick for most of his life. He often rode the ferry to Algiers. Paxton knew just about everybody on that ferry.

"Yes, sir."

"No need for sir. You know me."

"Yes, Mr. Williams."

The recruiter looked him up and down. "How old are you? Fifteen?"

"No sir, I'm eighteen. Gonna graduate in six months."

"Well, we can take you right now, but hadn't you oughta get your diploma first?"

Paxton thought about it. "I guess so."

"Of course so. You'll have a lot more freedom to forge your path in life with that diploma. What if the Merchant Marines don't suit you?"

"But sir, I know I'm a sailor."

"I've known you for years, kid. I won't have your mother come after me with a billy club for yanking you out of high school. Hold on and be patient. Besides, if you ever want to hold a rank, you'll need that diploma so you can go to the academy."

Paxton agreed. Mr. Wilson watched the boy's plump

bottom wiggle as he walked out of the recruitment center. He blew a long wolf whistle once the kid was out of earshot. He muttered to himself, "He's gonna be real busy on that boat."

2
A LIFE AT SEA

Paxton spent the remaining months until graduation studying textbooks about sailing, flags, maritime laws, terminology, and anything else he could find. He let his mother know about the plans; she was upset for herself but happy he had found his calling. "Not every man figures out who he's gonna be. You can see those lost souls on Poydras Street, sleeping against the sides of the buildings. If you choose a life at sea, I pray you will never be amongst them."

"Thanks, Ma." He kissed her cheek.

She struggled with the next bit. "Honey, you don't know it yet, but you're special."

"Special? How so?"

She studied her nails. "Your daddy, he came to me because he was afraid he couldn't please a lady or have children. It turned out he didn't want a baby, and a lady couldn't please him none, either. He wasn't the marrying kind. I got a hunch you're like your daddy; you're not going to be happy with a lady."

Paxton frowned. "I don't follow you." Did having a baby matter? He wasn't sure he wanted one.

She smiled. "You'll figure it out on the open seas. The thing is, you need to know that I love you no matter who you become. So be who you are. Please just remember that. Don't fear me none; I love you."

Paxton was deeply confused. He had no idea what she was trying to tell him. He found out soon enough.

◈

THE DAY AFTER GRADUATION, DICK WILLIAMS GAVE Paxton his uniform and dungarees wrapped in blue laundry paper tied with string. It was starched until it was board-stiff. With his life's possessions in a duffel bag, he climbed the gangway of the tramp ship MV Southern Cross. He made his way downstairs to the mariner's quarters. Because he was new, he was all the way at the bottom of the boat. He counted room numbers as he walked down the passageway. Like a Hollywood musical, sailors poked their heads out of the open doors as he walked by. Paxton held out hope that one of those heads belonged to the man with the ocean in his eyes, the green carnation on his wrist, and the snake in his pants. He was too innocent still to recognize that yearning. All he knew was that he longed again for that firm but gentle hand on his backside. He mistook the longing as a desire to be friends. It was more.

Every head that popped out belonged to a handsome sailor, but none of them was that blue-eyed sailor who had been so kind to him. Of course, in a sea afloat with a thousand ships, the odds were small that he would be aboard. And he wasn't.

The whistles of appreciation were vexing. Paxton had no clue that what God stole from him in front, he bestowed to perfection elsewhere. His face could start wars, and his ass was a fistfight. He got his beauty from his mother. But that butt was the most perfect, heart-shaped mound of flesh ever to walk the deck of any ship.

He found his room: ST-4. It was cramped. It didn't

help that his bunkmate sat on the top bunk, smoking a cigarette and glaring at Paxton like he was a dirty floor. Paxton put on his charm and extended his hand. With a smile, he said, "Paxton Smalls, new recruit."

The sullen roommate reluctantly held out a hand and said, "You can call me Brick."

Paxton appraised his new bunkmate. He had curly, red hair, unkempt. A thin mustache covered his lip. He had two dark circles under his eyes, just above his freckled nose and cheeks.

Brick admitted he looked like crap. "I've been on this ship too long, Paxton. I'm not much of a welcoming committee." He cracked a smile that made him a lot younger. "Hey, let me show you around."

They started with the room. "I'm top bunk, and there is no arguing it. You're a cadet, so live with it." Paxton couldn't see why he should care. The bottom bunk meant he had a smaller distance to fall in a storm, and less hassle to the toilet.

Brick pointed to the desk and rolling chair. "That's for writing letters home and blow jobs." Paxton didn't remember reading about blow jobs in his textbooks. He figured it was some kind of navigation chart.

"Where's the toilet?"

"Down the hall. There's one head for twelve mariners. I would show you, but there's no need; you can't miss the smell."

They ascended the stairs to the non-com deck. This was where the cooks, the engineer, and the bo'sun stayed. The mess was on this level. "You only get sandwiches while we're in port. Once we're on the open sea, breakfast is at 5:30 am. Lunch is noon. Dinner is at 5:30 pm. You get about 15 minutes to eat, so don't be late."

Paxton was taking notes. He dropped his pen. Bending over to pick it up, he caught Brick licking his lips.

"What?" Paxton still had no idea.

"A boy as pretty as you, with an ass like that - you're going to spend a lot of time in the barrel."

"I don't know what you're talking about."

Brick narrowed his eyes. "Let's go back to the room where I can explain it in private."

"But we haven't seen the officer's deck."

"Later."

3

HIS FIRST ABLE SEAMAN

Back in the room, Brick was silent. He removed his shirt, then motioned for Paxton to do the same. They took turns until both men were in nothing but their underwear.

"You never done this before, have you?"

Paxton didn't know what it was, but he was sure he hadn't. He shook his head.

"You're in luck. I'm one of the best." Paxton was indeed lucky; Brick was a smaller-than-average man below the belt.

Brick had him bend at the waist so he could rest his torso on the desk. The freckled fingers tugged at his underwear. Oh no! He didn't want Brick to know his horrible secret. But he wouldn't find out with his face buried in his ass like it was now.

Brick sucked on Paxton's butthole like it would buy him a drink. The young seaman was initiated into the joys of ass-licking. The experienced man used his tongue to dig deep, then flexed it to stretch the boy's sphincter.

"Oh sweet Jesus!" Paxton pounded on the desk. "It ain't right something should be this good." He felt Brick nod even as he buried his nose deeper.

Five minutes more, and Paxton was as slick as an ice highway in July.

Brick pulled back. "That ought to do it."

Paxton figured things were done. He pulled his pants up.

"Hey, now, we're just getting started." Brick tugged the boy's dungarees from his grip and let them fall to his ankles. He saw Paxton's problematic penis.

"Damn. Most men prefer them small. You're gonna be a busy sailor."

Paxton rocked from one foot to the other. "But what about women?"

Brick shrugged. "Women ain't your concern. Not the way God made you."

"God fucked me over."

Brick smiled. "Bend over, and I'll teach you what it means to get fucked over."

A shiver went through him. He liked when Brick spoke to him like that. He leaned across the desk, sweating with fear and excitement.

It started off fine. It was harder than the tongue, but gentle. Then a blinding pain choked off all other thoughts. "Oh! Shit, that hurts!"

Brick backed up an inch. He knew his way through virgin ass. "You need me to stop, or can I keep going?"

Paxton waited, then, "Go on."

Brick pushed in hard, so his head popped past the tight spot. "Still okay?"

A nod was all he needed. With a fury, he pumped his little dick in and out a hundred times a minute. Paxton loved being fucked like a woman. He moaned and spread his cheeks to let Brick in deeper. The slamming continued. Paxton's legs quivered. He grabbed the edges of the desk to keep from falling. The quivering kept going. It lifted his mind twenty feet above. With his mind's eye, he could gaze down and see his roommate penetrating him with his little dick. It made the quivering increase.

"You like that, Pax?"

Nothing but a moan in response. Brick lay him on his back in the bottom bunk. From that position, Paxton could shake inside without falling. He watched his redheaded roommate fuck him. How could they both feel so good? Brick's grin looked just how Paxton felt. He wrapped his legs around his bunkmate and ran his hands across his chest.

Brick skipped a beat every time the boy's hand grazed his nipples. "Pax, you sly fox, you found my weak spot."

Paxton held on to both nipples. Brick's eyes were barely visible. He caressed the plum-shaped bottom as he plowed it.

"Shit, I'm gonna come!"

Paxton wondered what that meant.

Brick repeated his warning, then threw his head back. "Aaaaargh!"

The man's penis pulsed inside the lad's butthole. Was he peeing? No, it was thick. When Brick removed his softening penis, globs of the white goop came with it. They left a puddle on the wool blanket.

"Sorry about that, Pax. You can trade with me." They swapped blankets. Brick was snoring in minutes, but Paxton's thoughts were racing. So many comments and hints made sense now. He was built to please a man.

❧

PAXTON HAD TROUBLE WALKING THAT FIRST DAY AT sea. Sharp pains spread where his asshole muscles connected to his legs. Every step was uncomfortable, but he grew used to it. He carried his mop and bucket to the non-com floor. Scrubbing the deck, he attracted the attention of passersby. He heard a wolf whistle and whirled to stare at the Third Officer.

"Sir." He saluted.

"This ain't the real Navy, kid. At ease - permanently."

Paxton smiled. His face could melt butter. "Yes, sir. What brings you below?"

"After seeing your ass, I plum forgot."

A new sensation washed over him like a wave of hunger. He craved that quivering again. He studied the Third Officer's body. He was older, maybe 30 years old. He was over six feet tall. His uniform strained to hold in his muscles. His biceps had worn out the seams on the cuffs of his short-sleeved shirt. His chest threatened to pop a button at any moment. Paxton stole a glance below, and saw a big lump between those meaty thighs.

"Sir. You're so big."

The officer grabbed between his legs and grinned.

"Big all over. Name's Rocky. You must be Paxton."

Instead of shaking his hand, Rocky put his arm around the boy. "I'll bet you'd like to see how the officers live."

Paxton nodded.

❧ 4 ❧

HOW THE THIRD OFFICER
LIVES

Rocky had no roommate. Officers got their own bunk to themselves. There was a tiny cabinet in the corner labeled "Toilet." He had a sink to wash his face.

"Only the captain gets his own shower. I still have to bathe with the rest of you. Not that I mind. I like the camaraderie."

"I prefer to shower alone." Paxton said.

"There's only a dozen of us, so I'm sure you can find — I'm wasting time." He unbuttoned his shirt, revealing a tight undershirt that accentuated his nipples atop his massive chest. When he pulled off his white trousers, Paxton gasped. Rocky didn't wear underwear. He had a man-sized cock. Much bigger than anything Paxton had seen. It was slowly unsticking itself from the side of his leg until it dropped in front. It pulsed as it grew bigger and lifted off his balls.

"Come on, don't leave me hanging!"

Paxton blushed with shame. When he finally shucked his boxer shorts, Rocky saw his insignificant endowment. "You're a real pleaser. I love it."

"How can I please anyone with this?" He gestured towards his worthless appendage.

"You can't. It's your ass. You were designed for men

like us." He grabbed his swollen cock. "It's our job to give you as much pleasure as we take from you, or more. Just like we do with a woman."

Big tears filled Paxton's eyes. He said, "I'm not a woman."

"Hey, Hey. What's this?" The Third Officer held Paxton close. Paxton was safe nestled between Rocky's enormous pectoral muscles. "Sit here." He made a thick chair out of his furry thigh. Paxton held on to Rocky. He smelled of cologne and the sea. His burly arms held him tight. He had never known a father's embrace, but he knew this was it.

There was brisk knock at the door. "Captain called an all hands meeting at 1300 hours. You got 30 minutes."

Paxton sniffled. "I guess I had better go."

"Oh come on, I can get you begging for more in ten minutes."

He carried the boy to his bed. With his legs aloft, Paxton could see Rocky aim his big dick at his sore ass.

"Here." Rocky handed him a tiny tube of glass covered in canvas webbing. "Break this and inhale."

"What is it?"

"It's a shortcut."

Paxton broke the vial, and after inhaling the fumes, fell back on the officer's bunk. Blood pounded in his ears. His heart pounded against his ribs. His vision went blurry. Somewhere very far away, something slippery led to something much too large. There was pain, but the way Rocky's cock filled him was different than Brick. The big cock was more comfortable, stretching out his sides instead of poking them. He thought of a stuffed turkey.

As Rocky pistoned in and out, he hit a few spots that Brick could not. They made the young sailor's insides shake.

"Am I too rough?" Rocky's sweat cascaded onto him.

"Not rough enough, sir."

Rocky doubled the pace. He fucked in long, cruel strokes. Paxton inhaled hard when Rocky pressed up against a spot about five inches deep, and it made the trembling triple. He looked down, shocked to see his tiny penis drooling a clear mucus. Rocky caught the juice in his palm and ate it.

"The fountain of youth." Rocky spoke between heavy breaths. "Here." He held his cupped palm to Paxton's mouth and forced him to taste. It was sweet.

"I'm gushing the same stuff inside you right now, son. It'll put hair on your chest."

Whatever lubricant Rocky had used made the pain bearable. The thought of that big fat cock drooling in his ass made Paxton gush another puddle of sticky liquid.

"You like it, don't you son?"

Paxton grinned. "Yes, Daddy."

The word was explosive. Rocky's muscled ass was a blur as he drove himself deeper, finally hitting a wall. The wall hurt Paxton at first, but it became a source of even more pleasure as the beating continued.

"You like it when Daddy fucks you with his big cock, don't you?"

Paxton nodded.

"Daddy's gotta finish."

The clock showed it was nearly 1300 hours.

Paxton grabbed the nipples nestled in fur atop giant mounds of muscle. He squeezed them gently.

"Harder! Pinch Daddy's titties hard, son." Rocky's dominance was like rum to Paxton. Following orders was so much easier than thinking for himself. He twisted and pinched. Rocky opened his eyes wide.

"I'm gonna come."

Paxton knew it was time, but he wanted this to last forever. Rocky lifted him at the waist. "Oh son, your ass was made for Daddy's dick."

Paxton leaned forward and put Rocky's left nipple in his mouth. He sucked and chewed like it would give milk.

"Oh shit!" Rocky's muscular body nearly doubled in size as every muscle flexed. Paxton loved Rocky's white butt. He pressed on it, encouraging Rocky to stay deep.

"I'm there; I'm there, son."

"Come in me, Daddy."

Rocky's huge balls released a hot thick flood inside Paxton. He squirted much more come than Brick had, and for a lot longer. The muscular officer cradled the boy in his arms for half a minute.

"Bathroom, now! Empty that hole and get on deck, son."

"Yes, Daddy."

"You say 'yes sir' until I tell you otherwise. Now go shit my come out and get ready."

Paxton was startled to see his blood mixed in with the tablespoon of Rocky's semen he expelled.

❈   5   ❈

WORKING THE HOLYSTONE

The whistle blew 1300 hours. Paxton was still buckling his belt when he reached the Officer's quarters. He thought he heard a few snickers. Rocky had beat him by twenty seconds tops. They were both covered in sweat. The assembled crew were an odd sight. There was Rocky and Brick, of course. But he had not yet met the others. A few were dressed casual. From his reading, he knew this must be the non-coms and the chefs. There were mariners like him. Some were Able Seamen, AS like Brick, with the full uniform. Others like Paxton were OS, Ordinary Seamen in starched dungarees and a denim shirt. Every last one of the crew were rugged, handsome, and cheerful. It was like Paxton wanted to eat a whole box of Nilla Wafers. It was hunger for something other than food. He was waking up to his erotic desires.

The captain was brief. He introduced the newest member of the crew, Paxton, and said their next port of call would be Havana in 48 hours. As a "tramp" steamer, the Southern Cross went wherever demand dictated, often on very short notice.

Paxton returned to the non-coms deck to continue swabbing. It was hard to ignore the way men walking by watched his butt like a wolf watching sheep. Paxton grew up believing he was a real man. This new situation showed him how unlike a man he really was. He was a receptacle for other men to use, like a Kleenex. The tears returned, stinging his eyes and making it nearly impossible to do a good job on the deck. His denim shirt was spotty with tears and snot. He was so angry at his mother for giving birth to him with a half-man for a father. He didn't yet appreciate all the blessings God had bestowed instead. He didn't know that his ability to take pleasure from anal penetration was rare. He had yet to discover the rarest gift.

Rocky pulled Paxton off the holystone and gave him the easy task of inspecting the ropes and cables for any worn out rigging needing replacement. The work was simple, yet it required intense concentration. Several hours went by in the blink of an eye. It was hot and humid, so the young sailor drank in large gulps from his canteen. He soon needed to pee.

He went to the toilet. It was empty, thank god. Then at the urinal, another OS stepped up beside him and pulled out a small but perfectly functional penis. Paxton was afraid to reveal his. He knew he couldn't stand there and wait, so he leaned forward and pulled out the button of flesh. Shielding his embarrassment from view, he sprayed the trough with his best aim, hoping he didn't hit the sailor next to him, who had taken a step back to display his little penis, which resembled a giant next to his insignificant nub of flesh. Paxton was still ruminating over his lot in life and didn't realize he was staring at the man's swelling cock. It was growing at an alarming rate.

"Damn it, Pax, now I can't pee!" The young man's penis had doubled in length and girth, and was still growing.

"I-I'm sorry. I wasn't- I mean it wasn't me."

The guy was not really mad. He just enjoyed intimidating the new arrival. "Look at it! It's so big and hard now because of you. I can't pee until you suck it. With strong hands, the OS pushed Paxton into a stall. Sitting down hard, Paxton wasn't sure what was happening.

"Name's Bill, by the way, but folks are starting to call me Trip, so you can too."

"Are you the third Bill in your family? Is that why they call you Trip?"

"Nah, it's because I triple in size when I get hard."

Trip held the large chunk of meat in front of Paxton's mouth, and clubbed his nose with it a couple times. "Open your mouth."

"Don't you want my ass?"

"Hell no! I don't stick this beauty in the mud. Just mouths and pussies,"

Paxton feared this would end badly. Trip put his swollen cock into Paxton's mouth and pushed it to the back of the throat. Paxton coughed up phlegm.

"That's the way." He started doing to Paxton's throat what Brick and Rocky had done to his ass. He held the boy's head and forced himself in and out in a slow cadence. It made Paxton retch at first, but the rhythmic motion calmed his reflexes until he could take the whole thing down his esophagus. Of course his airway closed when it was jammed full of dick, so Paxton had to hold his breath for long stretches.

"Wow, you are a natural." Trip's compliment made him blush. He liked being used by men like Trip: arrogant, pushy and well hung. He didn't care if it made him less of a man.

"Ready for fourth gear?"

Paxton couldn't nod with a long stiff cock in his throat. "Mm-hmm."

Trip sped up to a blinding rate. His cock was flying so fast and so far down Paxton's throat, he couldn't get enough air.

Trip's eyes were closed. Pax tapped in vain on his throat rapist's legs, stomach, butt...nothing. Trip was deep in his head somewhere, pounding Paxton's mouth like it was wet pussy.

The edges of Paxton's vision turned red, and the red marched slowly to cover his eyes completely. Just before he passed out, he tasted a hot salty flood in his mouth and throat. It tasted like gumbo.

He awoke in a few moments to Trip slapping his face. "Wake up! Jesus why didn't you tell me?"

It hurt to speak. "My mouth was full." He sounded like a chain smoker.

Trip scurried off to wherever he belonged, and Paxton returned to the cables. In that whole encounter, never once did he reveal his pitiful wiener. Trip didn't care. He just needed somewhere to shove his own glorious meat. Paxton was ashamed that he liked it. He was ready for more. But he was inferior, being a woman to these men. He knew what his mother did, and he didn't want to be like her. She got paid for it; Paxton didn't. Did that make it better or worse?

The noontime fuck with Rocky had left Paxton starving without lunch. The creole gumbo Trip fed him was hardly a meal. Dinner was just an hour away. He was done with his work. It was time to go below deck and consider who he was and what he was becoming.

❧ 6 ❧

A LONGING FOR SIZE

Brick was happy to discuss it with his new roommate. "Pax, you see, you're never, ever going to be able to fuck a hole, so just get that notion out of your head. You're too little."

Paxton groaned. He wanted to curl up and die. Brick continued. "Every ship has one. It's the guy with the smallest willy. He spends all his time in the barrel. Hell, I've been that man before. Believe me, I was sore every day on that ship. You're lucky we're not all hung like horses."

Paxton thought of the horses at Jackson Square and remembered their huge cocks. He shivered.

"I have never seen one as small as yours, so it won't matter what ship, you're going to spend all your time in the barrel for the whole crew."

Paxton was defeated. "I'm doomed."

"Doomed? Are you saying you didn't like it?"

"Well, yeah, I mean, no, it was great. I just feel so dirty for liking it. But is was heaven."

"That's because you were blessed with that ass. It's wired for pleasure."

"It hurts a lot now, though."

Brick smiled, "I know. But once you get past that, there's nothing better in the world." He picked up a two-day-old copy of the Times-Picayune and read the Sports section.

Paxton reflected on his experiences, all of them new and different. It was true; once the pain subsided, it was the most satisfied he'd ever been. Brick was good, and big Rocky was great. He even enjoyed Trip fucking his throat. Something was still missing though. Was it size?

"Hey Brick?" The redhead put down his newspaper.

"Yeah, buddy?"

"I like big ones."

Brick shrugged. "That leaves me out. Why don't you try George the cook?"

"Is that the Mexican one?"

Brick shook his head. "No, actually, George is Portuguese. I've never seen it, but it's legendary. Oh, and of course Captain Alder. You won't believe your eyes."

"He's big?"

"A colossal hunk of meat. You need to work your way up to it. Start with George a few times, then see the captain. To be safe, before George you might want to practice a while on someone a little less...intimidating."

"Like who?" Paxton was taking notes.

"Look at you, a little size queen. It's a pity they'll wreck your hole for the rest of us."

"Wreck...my hole? Can they do that?"

"Well, it gets looser. It starts to look like a pussy after a while. So yeah, someone in between."

"Like Rocky?"

Brick guffawed. "I see you already met. He's got size. Rocky's big, but not the kind that leaves you inside-out with pussy lips." He stroked his thin whiskers. "I know."

"Who?"

BRICK'S PROPOSAL

B rick led Paxton to the officer's deck, to Rocky's room.

"I thought you said—"

"Hold up." Brick knocked. Rocky came to the door in pajama bottoms. He filled them out well.

"Come in."

A few minutes later, Paxton was in Rocky's lap, face to face. The Officer's cock was buried deep inside him. He wondered what Brick was doing behind him. It didn't take long to find out. Brick pushed his way in. Pax howled with the pain of two cocks inside him at the same time.

"Shh, Shh." Brick said. "It won't hurt for long."

Paxton shook with pain. His legs wobbled, even as he was supported by Rocky's hairy, ham-thick thighs.

The officer put his lips to Paxton's. Their tongues caressed each other. Brick leaned in from behind and stole a backward kiss. It was just a peck. Then Rocky held Brick's head, exploring his mouth with his long tongue. They had a history together; it showed. Being the hole that glued these two cocks together was a privilege. As Brick pushed closer to the officer, his small cock rubbed against the much bigger pole. Both men shuddered with delight.

Paxton, wedged between them, had a few body shivers of his own. Between the pressure of Rocky's cock against the deep recesses of his rectum, and the hole stretching combination of cocks at the entry, he was in his own bubble of pleasure. The fucking grew more intense. Brick fell out several times, but he popped right back in. Rocky strained to get his brawny arms to reach Brick. When he did, he put his hands on the redhead's freckled ass and pulled him closer. Paxton was pressed hard between the men. He rocked his butt in time with the double-fucking. He stared at Rocky's hard nipples mounted on two big flesh mountains. He lowered his head and sucked hard.

Rocky jerked from the sudden burst of pleasure. His cock hit the magic spot; Paxton leaked pre-come all over the muscle-man's belly. Rocky knew the spot now. He pushed and pushed, milking the lad's tiny nub and sharing the sweet syrup with both men. The two top men grew dizzy from the hormone-laden sap. It was really true; Paxton was like a different type of man from the others. He didn't ejaculate; he only dribbled the clear precome. Maybe he was part woman. The thought revolted him. He focused again on pleasing the two studs fucking his ass.

Rocky was first. He looked about to sneeze. "Shit guys, here it comes."

The come made the long journey from his balls out the head to the end of Paxton's rectum. It was a lot. Gravity brought it raining down on Brick's little pecker. The hot juice made him slip and slide along the base of Rocky's massive shaft, He pounded hard. "Damn this is it. Fuck I'm coming!" Brick spewed sperm upwards inside the stuffed hole, mixing his essence with the officer's. Their cocks softened and slipped out of the boy's ass. A waterfall of come showered down on the two limp cocks.

When Paxton pushed out the last drops, he lifted off of Rocky's thick thighs.

Brick suggested a second round, but Rocky pointed to the clock. It was nearly 2100 hours. Time to sleep. Havana tomorrow.

On the way down the two flights of stairs, Paxton's legs shook. He staggered. Brick draped the boy's arm across his shoulder and put his own arm around his waist to steady him.

"Was that good?"

Paxton nodded. "That was great."

Brick beamed. "We can arrange a few more like that before you graduate to the giant ones."

❈ 8 ❈
HAVANA

At breakfast, Paxton fidgeted in his seat. His ass wasn't ready to sit on a hard bench just yet. A few seamen chuckled. They must know what happened. He looked at Brick, who didn't seem to notice or care.

He looked up from his eggs. "Pax, I'm letting you know ahead of time. I gotta go ashore in Rio, so there'll be someone new in the room."

"Who?"

"I don't know, but I'll bet it's Erasmus."

"Erasmus. Tell me more about --"

Brick interrupted, "Later. You gotta holystone the deck before Havana."

"Have you been to Havana?"

"Yeah, it's swank."

After scrubbing the heck out of the deck with holystones, the men were relieved to hear the blast that signalled the arrival in Havana harbor.

From the murmurs, Paxton knew it was break time. He, Brick and Rocky went ashore. Paxton was still sore from the double fucking they had given him. He struggled to keep up. They bought cigars, a Coke and a bottle of rum, then found an open bench on the Malecon. The island of Cuba had many different races.

There were a lot of black people, but there were also people of Spanish descent, Creole, and Blond-haired men from god knows where. The parade of handsome men and beautiful women passing them was as intoxicating as the rum and Coca Cola. They started with sips from each bottle, then gradually emptied the cola into the rum.

Paxton had never tasted anything so sweet and delicious. The cigars were foul smelling but the effect, once Paxton learned how to puff, was another layer of glee imposed on the drunken rum. Rocky popped off and came back with hot pork sandwiches with pickles and melted cheese. It was no po' boy, but it was still pretty damn delicious.

By nightfall, the trio stumbled aboard the Southern Cross. Paxton was sure they would be in trouble, but looking around, it was clear they weren't the only ones indulging in rum. The steam whistle blew three times, and they were out of the harbor, headed for the island of Tobago.

Rocky went to his cabin to sleep off the rum. The two roommates tripped down the stairs and landed in the bottom bunk together.

Brick held Paxton's perfect face in his rough hands. "You are beautiful."

"Don't you mean handsome? I'm a man!" He scowled.

"Handsome is common. Beauty - that's a gift from God. You are beautiful." Brick stroked the boy's cheek, then leaned in for a real, romantic kiss.

Brick may be small, but he had a smooth technique. In one motion he pulled down his own pants and also exposed Paxton's rump. It was painless when Rocky entered him. It was only because he liked to see Brick happy that he enjoyed the sex. His penis was small and insufficient. Paxton needed a big cock in his ass. With

Brick he was eating potato chips when he could be having steak.

Brick was drunk, but he still had good technique. Paxton enjoyed momentary bursts of pleasure when Brick poked him the right way. The sex ended with Brick shooting his load across Paxton's body, coating him like a glazed donut.

❧ 9 ❧

THE MORNING AFTER

In the morning, a few minutes before breakfast, Paxton woke to find he had slept on Brick's chest all night. His neck and back were stiff, but Brick's smile loosened it all up for him. Paxton traced circles around the freckled nipples and got strong squeezes in return. He couldn't see himself, but if he could, he would see a youth so beautiful, he made most women look haggard by comparison. Brick kissed him softly one, two, three times on the lips.

"I'm going to miss those lips when I'm gone."

"Why do you have to get off in Rio, Brick?"

"My old lady phoned ship-to-shore. She's in a family way and she needs me there."

Paxton stiffened. He didn't know Brick was married. "It was you that got her pregnant?"

Brick did math in the air, counting backwards. "Yep, that was the time."

Paxton rubbed some of the dried semen from his neck. "You're wasting this on me?"

Brick could see his bunkmate was agitated. He knew what would settle him down.

"Let me show you something," he said.

Brick knelt down and put Paxton's tiny cock and

balls in his mouth. The younger man stiffened -- embarrassed and intrigued in equal measure.

"Wha- What are you doing, Brick?"

Brick's mouth was too busy to answer. He stopped licking the miniscule meat to ask, "Do you like it?"

In answer, Paxton moaned. He pushed Brick's lips back onto his tiny cock, leaned back on his elbows, and let the redheaded stud do his work.

'This must be what fucking would feel like,' he thought to himself, 'If I ever could fuck.'

Brick detoured and licked the inside of Paxton's thigh. He massaged it with his lips, sending shivers through him. He licked the perineum, applying pressure.

Paxton suddenly needed to piss - much more urgently than usual. He pulled Brick away from his crotch. The redhead leaned in and kissed him, but Paxton pushed him away.

"Brick, I gotta pee real bad." Even as he said it, the urge was subsiding.

The experienced sailor was puzzled. "Pax, have you ever shot your load?"

"I can't, it's not big enough."

"Who told you that? Look, I promise, if you have to "pee", you just let loose in my mouth, on my head, anywhere you need to do it." He went down again, licking and flicking the tiny penis.

Immediately, the urge to pee came back. Paxton panicked. "Oh fuck, Brick, I'm gonna pee now."

Brick nodded. He kept tonguing the nub of flesh, then put it in his mouth like a nipple. His tongue circled and sucked the tiny sex organ.

Paxton prayed he wouldn't pee in Brick's mouth. He was groaning and fighting it. Suddenly, there was no holding back. But what came next wasn't normal - It was like he was inside a cotton candy machine. His breath heaved, and his asshole twitched. Brick pulled back to let him see. A fountain of white sperm shot out of his tiny penis, hitting Brick in the eye. But there was more. He drew his breath and another load sprayed Brick's hair, face, neck and chest. It kept coming. The third shot was the biggest yet. After that, the contractions in his ass grew less frequent, and the pumping from his little balls shot smaller drops of come. Brick sucked the last of it out of the young sailor's dick. The two men grinned at each other.

"Damn, boy, where do you hide it all?"

Paxton blushed. "Did I just come?"

Brick nodded. He grabbed him and pulled his lips to his. They kissed like lovers. Paxton held back the tears. He didn't want to lose the first man he gave his ass to. He couldn't believe he could come like other men, despite his curse. If he let go of Brick, the man would see the tears. Paxton did his best to man up. When he regained control of his emotions, he let go. It was after 5:30, and they both needed a shower.

❧ 10 ❧

GEORGIE

They got to breakfast with a minute to spare. Brick picked up his plate of eggs and poured half of them into his mouth and the other half fell on the floor. Paxton had been cutting and stuffing them in small bites. He laughed and tried to pour the eggs down his throat like his friend and bunkmate, getting most of it on the floor. Out of the corner of his eye, he saw George, the Portuguese chef, scowling at him for making a mess.

"Don't worry, George, I'll clean it up." And he did. All morning they scrubbed the deck with holystone. It was tedious, but it worked. They broke for lunch, famished. When Paxton got in line for his chicken fried steak with mashed potatoes and gravy, George was serving. The OS couldn't read the chef's intentions. He was learning fast, though. He dropped a green pea and turned to bend and retrieve it. When he handed it to George he said, "I'm sorry, George. Can you throw it away?"

George smirked and tossed the offending vegetable into the trash. "I like it when you clean." His accent was thick. "It is, eh, better than the men."

Paxton smiled sweetly. "Thank you, George. I don't mean to be a bother."

George smiled back. "No bother, rapaz. My name is Jorge, not George."

Paxton tried to pronounce the Portuguese version of his name back. "Georgie."

"Close. No matter. You call me George."

Trip was next in line. "Come on! Can you two love-birds move it along? The rest of us got to eat!"

Paxton sat where he could eat and gaze at George. Brick and Trip joined him.

"You're playing with fire, son." Trip said. "There is nobody on this ship who could take him. Brick, you tried, right?"

Brick nodded. "Paxton's been practicing."

Paxton was enjoying the power he had over George, and hardly noticed the two men chattering at his side. He dropped his napkin strategically to give George another view of his magnificent heart-shaped buttocks. When he turned around, George was stroking himself under his apron. There was no way to see what he had under there, but legends always contain truth.

The Southern Cross picked up a two-part tramp voyage first to Tobago then on to Fortaleza in Brazil. It was a long haul with a lot of time at sea. Some sailors welcomed the long stretches; others complained about the delay in getting to Rio.

At dinner, Paxton continued his seduction of George. There was no more work to be done on his shift, volunteered to help George with the dishes. After supper, a dozen plates at a time, Paxton ran the tiny dishwasher. He and George dried plates together, each one stealing glances at the other. George was not terribly handsome; he was tall and stout. A five-o'clock shadow helped hide some of the imperfections in his skin.

Paxton knew better than to break a dish, so he let a spoon fall. Bending for it, he felt George caress his bottom. He stood back up and smiled. "That was nice, George. Do it again."

He allowed George's paws to roam, stopping when they got to his crotch. He retreated, staying above his waistline, rubbing up under the young sailor's shirt. Paxton ground his butt into George. He gasped at just how enormous George was. He doubted his abilities. He should have practiced longer with Brick and Rocky. Based on what he was rubbing against, he should have found a third cock for their party to prepare him. No matter. He was in for a penny, in for a pound. Several pounds. A real pounding.

They retreated to the pantry. George stacked two sacks of flour and coaxed Paxton to bend over them. His sweaty hands spread lard in the tight butthole. Paxton couldn't see George, and when he glanced over his shoulder, George gently turned his head forward. "Is better if you don't see yet."

Paxton was scared. He shook visibly.

"Okay, we quit." George sighed, ready to wrap things up.

Paxton reached behind and grabbed George's meat. It was slicked up with lard. "We're doing this, George."

The man's enormous cock slipped from the his grip and thumped on the flour sack, raising a small dust cloud.

"No, you don't want this." George lingered, clearly needing to fuck.

"Put it in me slow." The young sailor spread his legs further apart.

The pain was bearable when he first put the tip in. Paxton still had not seen it, so he couldn't predict what was coming. It spread like a fire down the nerves in his rectum and perineum. Paxton suppressed a scream; it came out a yelp.

"I'm hurting you. We stop." George pulled out

"No, we don't stop. Fuck me, goddammit."

When George put it in a second time, it hurt a little less. But then he went further, and he got thicker, and the same scream rose to Paxton's throat. He turned it into a moan this time.

"I'm hurting you?"

"No, oh sweet Jesus it feels good." Paxton lied. After that very thick middle, the rest of George's cock slid in easily. The pain was everywhere, but Paxton grunted, moaned and made any sound he could to convince the Portuguese lunk to keep pressing forward. Soon, Paxton felt the tickle of the man's balls against his buttocks. His rectum was too full, the cock had nowhere to go, but he kept begging.

"All the way, baby, all the way. Oh right there. Right there."

With a pop, George's cock turned a corner and entered Paxton's sigmoid colon.

"Oh shit! Oh shit! Oh dear lord that does the trick!" It was like all the pressure had been released at once. The head of George's cock thrust its way deeper into the digestive tract before it finally stopped with George's legs between Paxton's, his pelvic bone pressed against the entryway to his ass.

"I'm okay to keep going?" Sweet George was so polite.

"Fuck me hard! And get in there deep!"

George knew how to fuck hard. He searched out the loosest women on the waterfronts of the cities. They could handle him halfway in their vagina, but he knew how to go deep all the way in the ass, where half his cock didn't have to remain out in the cold.

Given George's reticence up to this point, his powerful fucking took Paxton completely by surprise. The man thrust in long strokes, dragging the extra thick middle portion past the prostate and out the rectum before plunging back in again all the way until the head was nestled in the colon.

Paxton's fear dissolved into ecstasy. He knew all at once that this was his real gift. He could pleasure the titanic cocks and still receive pleasure in return. It took time to get started, but now that the cook was pounding and stretching him brutally, the sailor knew he had found his calling. Taking huge cocks was his mission in life. And right now, he was fulfilling the biggest mission yet.

"Pax, you soft like girl." George reached up and rubbed the tiny penis. But instead of shrinking from the touch, the young sailor put the older man's gnarled hand on his weiner. The pleasure coming from his ass was spreading to this little appendage.

"George, rub me."

"I lick a finger." He wet his hand with saliva and slid back and forth over Paxton's tiny hard penis and shrunken balls.

Paxton's eyes rolled back in his head. First, he leaked a tablespoon of clear juice that he produced every time the thickest part of George's cock passed his prostate. Then when that thick part left his ass and went back in, his legs trembled. When the head popped past that corner, he felt that need to pee, or come as it were, building. And George's slick finger intensified the urge.

George was making grunts of his own. He stroked the boy's little nub with care, like he did to the clitoris when he was buttfucking a whore in port.

For a huge hung man, he had a hair trigger. The right combination of excitement and touch set him off.

"I will come soon."

Those words gave Paxton intense satisfaction. Not only was he the sole reason this giant man was going to come, the man was making him come, too. It was the perfect negotiation where both parties win. He came down out of his head and to a building pressure in his crotch.

"I'm gonna come too, George."

George sped up the rubbing and twisting of the tiny cock and balls. It made him insane with pleasure.

"I come in your ass."

"Fill my ass with your come."

George reverted to his native tongue. "Porra! Tome a minha tubassa! Santa Maria!" The sound of cursing is universal, even if the words are not.

Paxton knew it was coming. "Shit, George, I'm gonna, I'm gonna!" And Paxton ruined the top sack of flour.

"Porra!" And then the giant came inside the young sailor. The head of his cock was so deep inside that Pax couldn't tell how much semen George had dumped in his ass.

George flipped him over onto his back, skewering him to the hilt.

George kept fucking. He still had more to push out.

"It's four months no sex. I go again, quick, I promise."

That was when Paxton realized that the downside of coming with a humongous cock in your ass was that the enjoyment diminished. As George's pounding wore on, the sex grew painful.

With an expert slicked up hand, George rubbed Paxton. At first, it was a struggle, but eventually those good feelings all came back. The joy of giving and getting pleasure in one act washed over him again, and he smiled. George smiled back. He stopped rubbing.

Paxton lifted his head to get a glimpse of what was going in and out of him with such pleasure. It was not a pretty cock. It was older, the pubic hairs had grey, but the dick itself was enormous. George had to stand with legs wide so he could make the long strokes. If he stood with his legs closed, he wouldn't be able to work the magic he was working now.

George's strokes made Paxton have a surprise

second orgasm with no hands. This time, the fresh sailor had an orgasm in his ass that traveled to his little cock. It didn't produce much sperm, but it felt good. George saw the little penis push out its load, and it sent him over the edge.

"I make you come. I come now." And that was all he had time to say. His whole body shook as he shot more sperm deep inside the young sailor's sigmoid colon.

George was unattractive, and his dick was ugly, but its size was enough to excite Paxton. As the cook softened and the serpent wound its way out of the hole, he revealed a massive piece of meat. He was mostly hard, and it hardly shrank as he got softer. It reached more than halfway to his knees, as thick as a mooring rope.

George was blunt, probably because of the language barrier. "I don't fuck boys. I make exception for you."

Paxton frowned. "You didn't like it?"

George sighed. "You don't have big titties. Not your fault. You get titties in Rio, I marry you."

Before Paxton could dig deeper into George's kinks, he farted. It was from all the air George had pumped into him. But then the fart turned into a stream of come. It was enough to fill a teacup. It leaked down onto the lower bag of flour. George laughed.

The big giant reached out to help Paxton to his feet. When he stood, he staggered. George caught him in an embrace. He didn't try to kiss him or hug him. He was just helping him get his sea legs back.

"Many women do the same when I am done."

"So, this is it?" Paxton wanted George inside him right now. He was so fucking huge.

"You grow some big titties and come see me again, yeah?" He slapped his bottom, which sent shockwaves of pain through Paxton's body.

"Sorry about the flour."

George laughed. "It's still good. Not to be preoccupied. I make biscuit and pancakes. Nobody know."

BISCUITS AND GRAVY

Brick was concerned when Paxton limped into their room.

"Little brother, are you okay?"

Paxton nodded. He felt like he'd taken a beating from a thug at school, but from the inside. His pain couldn't outweigh the excitement of the royal pounding that caused him to come all over the flour. He laughed to himself when he pictured everyone eating the biscuits and gravy in the morning. Brick hopped down off the top bunk and helped his friend into his bunk.

Brick stroked his hair. "Sleep it off, you'll be fine in the morning."

Morning came quickly. Paxton was no better than he had been when he stumbled out of the kitchen the night before. He limped upstairs to the mess. George scowled, but Paxton forced a bright smile. "Hey George. How's it hanging?"

George leaned forward in a conspiratorial whisper. "It's not. It's standing at attention." And it was. George kept it under the counter.

Paxton balked when the cook said, "Let's do it again tonight."

"But I didn't grow titties." He whispered.

"I don't care. Look at my dick." His apron was

loose, and you could still see he was hard as a rock and huge as fuck. "I need to be in you."

Paxton needed to come again like that. Only George had been able to make him ejaculate without touching his dick. Brick had a talented tongue, but he could never press him and stretch him enough to fill him up, a satisfaction one hundred times more powerful than a small dick in his entryway.

He and Brick had KP together. They peeled potatoes and talked about the upcoming battle inside his intestines. Brick was experienced. "There is no better cure for this than to do it again the next day," he said.

Paxton wrinkled his nose. "How is that possibly true? I'm bruised and probably torn up. Doing it again would only make it worse."

"It's different with ass fucking. The more you do it, the better it gets."

"You've never been with George!"

"No, but I've been with guys who were pretty close. Trust me, Pax. You will scream bloody murder the first minute, and then moan like a whore for the rest of the night."

Paxton's mom was a whore. He got pretty upset over Brick's choice of words, but it was the meaning behind them he heard.

"Brick, I'm not gonna back out of this, so you had better be right."

"Ten bucks says I am."

After sundown, Paxton met George in the pantry. He was so excited that his chef pants were ready to rip in two.

George dipped his hand in lard, and put a glob at the entryway. He lowered his pants with great effort, and his giant cock sprang up to his chest like a mouse-trap. He rubbed the lard up and down the length of his pole.

Paxton wavered between excitement and fear. He

kept Brick's advice in mind as George pushed his way in. It was much faster and more painful than the previous night. Paxton sobbed silently, certain he would die from the pain. If he let George know, it would stop. He grunted and whined, faking pleasure to keep the big Portuguese going. The grunts became moans and the whining ceased. To his amazement, he was no longer faking pleasure; he was overcome by it.

George planted his legs in the archer's stance and sunk his meat deep. He turned the corner and sent Paxton Into a shuddering orgasm-like trance. The big man was only just getting started. Brick had not been fibbing. After that first minute, it was better than before.

George plunged and retreated with the regularity of a sidewheel crank on a steamboat paddle. The long steady strokes put Paxton ever deeper into his trance. There was only pleasure, and hard flesh sliding against soft. When George pressed on the prostate, Paxton leaked clear sticky juice.

George smiled. "I know I do good when you come like woman." He let the clear juice fall and soak into the flour sack.

Paxton was angry that George spoke of him like a woman, but he was too turned on to stop. "You make my pussy wet."

George liked the dirty talk. "You want more wet?"

The novice nodded shamelessly. George went from steamboat to locomotive. Faster and faster he fucked. "I make you woman!" The cook grabbed onto Paxton's chest and squeezed until his nipples rose. "You have titties now."

George buried his face In the crack between Paxton's tits and licked it.

With George's cock hammering in and out of his gut, and the tongue on his breasts, Paxton began to moan in a higher pitch, like a woman. He became a dizzy girl, his cunt stretched wide by this man's hard, massive prick,

"Oh George, Come in my pussy."

"I gonna make you pregnant, yes, woman?"

"Put a baby in me."

George tried to do exactly that. His feverish pitch sent waves of intense pleasure through Paxton's insides. Somewhere at the base of his spine, a nerve throbbed in his minuscule genitals. "George, I'm gonna come!"

"Me too, pretty lady."

He squeezed the boy's breasts hard. Paxton responded by tightening his sphincter.

"A Porra!" George cursed with joy. "I come in you!"

Paxton didn't hear, he was busy having a full body orgasm. He shook from shoulder to toes. Again, without touching himself, he ejaculated multiple times, sullying George's apron and beard with his sperm.

"I make baby in you now!" George threw his head back and groaned. He released a giant shot of come.

"I'm going to have your baby."

Those words may have been responsible for the next five shots, each one progressively more than the previous. It was a milky white river of baby juice flowing into Paxton's colon.

George closed his eyes and awkwardly kissed Paxton.

Giddy with post-coital pleasure, the young man laughed. "I think your beard is going to get pregnant with my baby."

This sudden reversal of roles didn't please George.

In an angry retreat, he pulled his semi-hard cock out of Paxton's ass.

"You disgust me."

Paxton was shocked. "George, I didn't mean it. I'm the one getting pregnant."

"You are a man, you let me waste my seed in your cu."

Paxton began leaking the man's sperm out of his ass onto the flour sack.

"George, I..."

"Get out! Look at the flour. You filthy pervert."

The giant picked him up by the shirtfront and threw him towards the pantry door.

Paxton stood and left without a word. He heard George cry out, "Wait! I am sorry. Please!" He smiled to himself. He liked George best when he begged. As he went down the first flight of stairs, he was suddenly aware of how rough George had fucked him. His back hurt, and his rectum was on fire. Covering over the pain was a joyful tingling sensation. With each step, the pain and pleasure increased in tandem.

Doubled over, but tingling like a lightning strike, Pax stumbled into his bedroom. Grease and come trickled down his legs, soiling his pants. Brick smiled. "Did I win?"

Paxton nodded. "Ten bucks."

❧ 12 ❧

CAPTAIN ALDER

The next morning, George came to the cabin. Paxton rolled his eyes. "What?"

George cleared his throat. "I apologize for last night."

"Which part?"

"I yell and throw you."

"What about fucking me so hard? Do you apologize for that?"

George was stunned. "I don't...I am not apologizing for fucking you."

"And for treating me like a woman?"

"No, Paxton, I'm not sorry for that."

"Good. Then tonight you fuck me even harder and I'll scream like a woman for you."

Paxton made nightly visits to the pantry. George was a big oaf, but he knew how to make a man become a woman. Paxton wished they had more in common. The language barrier and lack of common interests were driving a wedge between them, so that the visits became pure sex and nothing else. It was George who asked for a break. Paxton needed him for sex, but he admitted defeat as far as a friendship was concerned. He agreed.

The next few days were torture. Paxton remembered alley cats yowling in heat back in New Orleans. He understood their pain. Brick did his best to help, but it was like being tickled with a feather. Even Rocky and Brick as a team couldn't do what George did. They were far more handsome and interesting, but they couldn't go to that place. Curious, Paxton went to the ship library to see if he could find an anatomy book. He found an illustrated dictionary. He searched until the word "bowel" revealed a map of the lower digestive tract. He saw the rough spots where Rocky had reached, called the rectal valves. George had turned the corner and went into the sigmoid colon. That explains why he thought he was poking a hole in his stomach.

On the third night without George, a knock came at the door. Pax hoped it was his well hung toy, but it was Captain Alder. If he came all the way down into OS territory, it meant someone must be in pretty serious trouble. The captain had broad shoulders draped with golden braids. His build was big, but not flabby. He was all muscle under that uniform.

"Young man, come with me."

They went up two flights of stairs to the Officer's Quarters, and then midship to the captain's Cuddy. He escorted Paxton into this most private room.

"I've heard about you and George." He said it so plainly, Pax couldn't tell whether this was a compliment or a disciplinary action.

"George is very well endowed. He has a rival., though."

The captain glanced downward and Paxton followed. What he saw couldn't be real.

"It's reserved for those who have demonstrated certain abilities."

Paxton studied the captain's face. He saw a twinkle.

"Can you handle it, son?"

"I really hope so."

And suddenly, the captain was upon him. He kissed the boy deeply. "Here, put your little paw on it."

Paxton placed his hand flat on the log in his pant leg. "It's big."

"No, grip it like this." Captain Alder curled the lad's fingers around the swollen mass, so thick that his fingers and thumb could not both touch the captain's leg at the same time. It stopped a few inches above the knee. About the same as George lengthwise but ridiculously thick, and growing thicker.

"I can't suck it."

"Nobody can. I had other activities in mind."

Paxton was desperate for a big cock in his ass, but not this sea monster. How could he possibly fit such a beast in his anus? It would tear him in two. He had that alley cat heat, much like a fiend for his dope or a drunkard his wine. He needed the captain inside him.

The cock had stretched the captain's white trousers to the point he could never get them off. Then the captain reached under the inseam and unsnapped the pant legs like a cowboy shirt. The colossal log fell out, causing Paxton to jump.

The captain chuckled. "You like 'em? I had a dozen of them custom made in Hong Kong. Damn near gave the tailor a heart attack."

"Sir, hadn't we ought to go to your cabin?"

"We're in the cuddy! My cabin is like Times Square. The cuddy is off limits to everyone on board. That includes you. It is invitation only."

The room had only a desk and a chair. Even flour sacks were better than this.

Captain Alder walked to a bare wall and pulled near the top molding. A Murphy bed unfolded.

The captain opened a desk drawer and removed a towel, a tub of Albolene, and a very thick rubber penis.

"Let's get you warmed up."

"What is that thing?"

The captain smiled. "It's called a dildo."

"What is it, though? Why do you have it?"

"These were invented by sea wives in Ancient Assyria to keep them from cheating during our long absences. I got this one in Maracaibo."

"But you're not married, so...?"

"So bend over and I'll show you how bachelors use them."

The older man coated the dildo in Albolene. It was thicker than George, but not as big as the captain. Paxton felt a familiar pressure against his anus. It grew more and more intense until at last the tight muscle gave way, accepting the whole rubber cock at once. The captain stumbled, caught off balance by the ease of forcing the tool into his belly.

"Damn, child. You're loose."

Paxton was in blinding pain, but didn't want the captain to know. As the man worked the rubber giant in and out, the pain subsided. The sensation of the rubber against his rectal walls was sublime.

After ten minutes of moaning and bliss, the captain removed the dildo. Breezes blew through Paxton's ass. He was gaping open like a cave.

Suddenly, real flesh and bone entered him. The captain put his whole hand inside. As the senior officer punched his way deeper, Paxton's hole stretched from wrist width to forearm size.

"How am I doing?"

"Good," Paxton lied.

"Perfect. Here comes the other one."

Paxton bit the nearest pillow to hold back the scream. Why was the captain doing this? He was thick, but not two forearms thick. The pain became transcendent. Nothing could stop the agony, so he embraced it and made it into a strange flavor of pleasure. His moans were genuine. He was dancing on the tightrope between agony and ecstasy.

"Turn around so I can see your smile."

Paxton rolled over. The captain's hands were in nearly to the elbows.

"Oh God. Oh sweet Jesus, dear lord." Paxton was mad at God, but he needed help to get through this.

"You're ready for me. I know that look." The captain removed his slippery hands and rubbed them dry on his enormous cock. He held open Paxton's gaping shitter and pressed his way in. To Paxton, it was a relief. Then he understood the captain's methods. He threw him in boiling oil so the boiling water would be an improvement.

"Not so bad, eh?"

Paxton nodded.

"Feels great down here, son." The older man was indeed well built. As the grey whiskers tickled Paxton's face, he felt the captain's powerful abdominal muscles working to guide and strengthen his thrusts. George was into women, but the captain liked young men. It made a big difference in his technique. Every stroke, every kiss, every prostate squeeze was engineered for mutual pleasure.

Paxton's bladder hurt. The captain was long enough, but far too thick to turn the corner. His blunt cock was a battering ram at the top of his rectum. It pushed hard into the surrounding organs, especially the bladder. Paxton struggled to be quiet and obedient.

"You don't like it?"

"It's great." Paxton hissed between clenched teeth.

The captain, encouraged, increased the pace and direction of his thrusts.

Paxton let out a howl. He was in a fog of pain and ecstasy.

"That's what I was waiting for!" The captain pounded his hole without relent. Paxton shrieked.

The pressure on his bladder was excruciating. He had to let go and allow the urine to exit his bladder before it burst. He pissed the bed a little, then tried his best to keep it from flooding.

"Did you piss the bed?"

Paxton nodded, bracing for the captain's fists.

But no fists came. The captain chuckled. "Every time. Don't worry, I planned for it."

The captain revealed rubber sheets under the cotton. "Just let it flow."

Paxton grew deeply ashamed as he wet the bed more and more. He hadn't done that since he was a young child. He struggled to hold back. With each thrust, the captain pushed more piss out.

Paxton let out a strangled cry that grew louder as the volume of urine increased. Finally there was nothing left.

"Ask anyone who's been with me. I fuck the piss out of 'em every time."

"Like who?"

The captain kept pushing and grinding into the sloppy hole. "Nobody on this voyage. They always seem to quit. You won't quit, will you?"

"N-n-no." The extreme pressure on his empty bladder was tolerable, if not a bit irritating.

"Good." The captain threw his head back and roared. "I feel it! Do you?"

Paxton nodded. He wasn't sure what "it" was, but he was definitely enjoying a lot of different things so chances were he did.

"I'm gonna come, Paxton Pisspillow."

Paxton wanted to punch the captain. He chose to moan appreciatively instead.

The captain's summer sausage meat stick swelled like a beignet in the fryer. With that final stretch, Paxton sensed something wrong inside. It was a knife of pain. The older man kept on thrusting, and the pain subsided. Then the captain spewed come. Because he was so thick, and he hadn't opened the passage to the colon, there was nowhere for the come to go but out the boy's hole. Come and blood sprayed all over the captain's sheets.

Panting, the officer covered the sailor with his muscular frame. His satisfaction was palpable. "Next time, it won't take so long."

Paxton saw the blood and felt faint. It was a lot more than he had guessed.

The captain groaned.

"Fuck. Fuck. Why do I do that? Sorry, Paxton. It's not as bad as it looks, I promise. You're not the first to bleed."

Paxton sighed. The gut punching had built a wall of misery, like a bruise being pressed hard.

After all that pain and struggle, he hadn't been able to get the captain past his rectum. He grew more lightheaded as he stumbled down to his room. He was too weak to open the door. When Brick answered, the lad tumbled into his arms. His pant seat had a bloodstain.

"Christ, Pax, are you all right?"

"Christ had nothing to do with it."

Brick held him tight, peppering him with kisses. "The captain did this to you?"

Paxton nodded. "It was glorious."

"He damn near killed you! Do you want me to report him?"

"No. It'll be better the next time."

Brick frowned. "I love you, man. Don't do this to yourself."

"I'm not your man. The captain claimed me."

Brick shook his head. "He can't do that."

Paxton shrugged. "He can if I let him."

CLAIMED

The next morning began with an argument.

"So I'm just a wife to you while we're out at sea?"

Brick laughed. "It's not that serious."

Paxton was furious. "You don't take me seriously?"

"Calm down, hot stuff. I'm not saying you're no good. Heck, you're probably better, but I got a family."

"But I have no choice. I'm either your woman or I'm nothing but a memory."

Paxton was purple. He wanted to punch Brick and every other normal man out there. He raised a hand; Brick grabbed it.

"Watch it, kid. What is this about?"

"You don't know what it's like! I have nothing at all down there."

"Don't you get it?" Brick asked. "You're built differently for a purpose. You'll make a lot of men very happy."

"But I want to be one of those men! I want to fuck your ass!"

Brick shrugged. "It ain't gonna happen. You're a jockey trying out for a fullback. Play to your strengths, man."

Paxton considered this. "I guess you know a little bit what it's like, being small and all."

Brick grinned, "Small gun, but full of bullets. I got two kids and a third on the way."

"I'm never going to have kids." Paxton hung his head.

"No, but you're going to have the best ass to ever sail the oceans, if the captain doesn't destroy it. You'll make Able Seamen tremble. You took George, for Christ's sake. You could make anyone happy. Maybe even Erasmus."

Paxton perked up. "What about Erasmus?"

"You'll see for yourself when we get to Rio. Let's just say he makes the captain look like me. And he pines for the pretty boys like you, but never can get one. He's just too damn big."

"Does his wife know?"

Brick guffawed. "Wife? Erasmus scares women away. He's a man's man. At least they try to take him. No one ever has. Lonely guy, really."

Paxton wondered how anyone could beat the captain. His insides were still bruised from the pounding.

Brick said, "Speak of the Devil, and he shall appear." It was the captain. He tilted his head in the direction of his cuddy. Without words, the two men had a conversation with their bodies. The captain wanted him; Pax was sore. Leading the youthful beauty by the neck, he commandeered him to the cuddy, his private room behind the wheelhouse.

Paxton lay on the bed and pulled his knees to is ears. The captain licked his lips. He pulled the young sailor to the edge of the bed. He wiped his bloody hole clean with a washcloth before lubricating him.

"Bit of a mess, eh? I'll be gentle this time."

But the captain's thick cock was incapable of being gentle. Paxton was glad. He liked it when this man was rough. He stuffed him full and used his powerful muscles to thrust and bludgeon his way to the back of the rectum, where he could go no farther. He left a good two inches exposed because he was too thick and hard to round the bend. Paxton pissed himself again but this time he got off on the pride in the captain's eyes.

"I'm fucking the piss out you again."

Paxton nodded. There was less blood this time. The ride was smooth, ending each thrust abruptly with a powerful kidney punch.

"Do you like your captain inside you?"

"Yes."

"Yes, what?"

"Yes, sir, captain, sir."

Paxton throbbed inside and out. It was pain, desire, lust and shame making a delicious sex soup in his brain.

He watched the captain's impossibly thick rod piston in and out of his anus. It was slick with jelly and shined in the tropical morning light. Paxton achieved that blissful Hindoo state of Kama, where all sensual pleasures intersect. The captain's masculine energies collided with the feminine spirit inside Paxton. Both men shook violently as the brutal colonizing cock conquered the fleshy rectal folds and pressed inwards, releasing an intense wave of pleasure not unlike female orgasm. Neither man ejaculated at that moment. They were overcome by the energy exchange. It was one perfect moment, and then it was gone forever. Neither man would share that bliss with the other again.

"Oh fuck, oh fuck, oh shit." The captain's flurry of epithets was followed by another powerful wave of release, and his cock shot hot white globs into The young sailor.

Paxton fired several rounds of come on the captain's bare furry chest. He felt the rapid withdrawal of the flesh log from his innards. His hole remained open, gaping like a foundering fish. The river of semen cascaded out, buttering the boy's thighs with the older man's juices.

A cold wind passed through the room. The captain tied his bow tie and adjusted the cap on his balding head. He smiled at Paxton. It was the smile of a pig farmer to his sow as he dreamed of bacon. It inspired dread.

"You have the day off, young man. I'm keeping this locked so you won't be disturbed. Oh, and this is for you." He dropped a packet on the dresser and left.

❈ 14 ❈

SOLITARY

Paxton spent a day of solitary confinement locked in the captain's cuddy, a diamond in a safe. The packet contained fifty dollars in fives.

The captain brought him breakfast, then lunch. They shared dinner. The captain showered him with kisses, but each one left Paxton colder than the last. When the captain unleashed his throbbing cock, Paxton obediently rolled over and let its immense girth and unrealistic length fill him completely. He moaned and pretended to enjoy it, just as his whore of a mother had done with the many uncles. He tolerated and even took pleasure in the violent pounding. It gave him a sense of belonging to a higher rank. But Paxton didn't come with the captain. The money bothered him almost as much as being treated like a possession. Neither of those marked the moment when he went from being loved to being owned. Instead it was that transcendent moment between them that had somehow closed the gates of Paxton's heart. It was gone. He loved the captain's huge cock and firm muscles. He loved to nurse on his big meaty nipples. He loved making extra money. But he didn't love the captain. He was a whore.

Pax lay awake beside the snoring captain. His insides were bruised and trembling. He thought back to the violent lovemaking, and realized for the first time that it wasn't mere size that would fill the emptiness. He needed something more. He struggled to find words for it. He touched the tender flesh on his behind. It hurt. What he needed was to hurt like that for someone who wanted them both to be happy. He knew such tenderness from Brick, but he would never be satisfied with a small penis like that. The captain had the right anatomy to fill him but only did it for himself. Brick hit the right place in his heart. He needed both.

Tobago was a mosquito-ridden spit of sand. Unlike Havana, there was very little to do. He rode alone with the "longshoremen" who pulled up to the boat. They had a dozen boatloads to bring out to the Southern Cross. It would be several hours. Walking down a shadeless drive, lined with grass shacks and discarded tires, Pax felt a deeper emptiness. They were only here long enough to pick up the sugar cane and plantains. In town, if you could call it town, he bought a Coca-Cola and realized why he was the only idiot who went ashore. The highlight of his time on the tiny island was lunch, served from a grass shack on stilts by a toothless old lady. It was lobster pie, and it was delicious. They accepted American coins here, so he bought two for a dime. He ate the second one on the way back to the ship. There was just enough room for Paxton to wedge himself between the cane and the plantains. He watched the clouds overhead as they moved rapidly by. In the distance, he heard thunder. Before he got to the ship, it was pouring. He tried to help the stevedores but they slapped his hands and sent him up on the crane with a load of cane.

He stepped under the metal overhang and removed his shirt. He wrung it out, but didn't put it back on. The captain saw him and ushered him to the cuddy.

"I don't want other men to see you half naked. They might get ideas.

Paxton nodded, seething inwardly. He used to believe the captain was the prize catch, but he was just an annoying prick with an inflated ego.

"You want to do it, then?"

The captain smiled. "I thought you'd never ask"

In the private room, the captain continued to give orders.

"Put your shirt on the radiator."

Paxton longed for Rocky the Third Officer, who treated him like a son, not a slave. But he had earned this, whatever it was worth. The attention of the captain was a valuable commodity, and lucrative too.

With military precision, the captain pulled out his cock and slipped it inside Paxton. It always hurt, but it took less time to find the pleasure now. He had very little time, so he was careless. He drew blood again, but didn't stop. He let his thick semen combine with Paxton's blood. When he withdrew savagely, the red and white mess flew out and stained the bedspread.

"God damn it!" The captain bellowed.

Paxton jumped with fear. But the captain wasn't a monster. He kissed him and apologized.

"Shall I clean it up, sir?"

"It's my mess, Pax, not yours. Just leave it."

Paxton's shirt was dry now, so he put it on. The fabric burned his skin. It was oddly pleasant. He was so loose, he couldn't hear his farts. His gaping anus expelled air, then come and blood that trickled down his leg.

Maybe the captain was a bit of a monster. "Clean that up!" His face glowed bright red.

Paxton had created a puddle on the hardwood floor.

"I don't have a rag."

"Use a washcloth, you worthless faggot!"

Paxton realized in that instant that despite being of low rank, he held all the power. The captain only got his way by yelling at him or ordering him about. But the captain needed Paxton, more than he needed the captain.

"Sir, I'd like you to clean it up." he stood defiant.

The captain raised his arm.

"Do it," Paxton said, "or you'll never fuck me again."

"What's this insolence?" He held his arm as though to strike.

Paxton gestured towards his gaping anus. "If you want this, you have to treat it right."

The Captain reddened, then said softly, "That's no way to talk to your captain. I don't want your ass, I own it. Now that disgusting mess is your fault, so clean it up."

"If the General Directorate inspects my torn asshole, who's at fault then?"

The color drained from his face. "You wouldn't dare." He lowered his arm. Paxton won.

"Clean up your filthy come. You put it in me, and it's not my problem it came out. Or leave it, I don't care."

The captain lowered his head. "You're right. I'm sorry." He went to the bathroom, his thick log swinging from side to side. Paxton watched him clean, enjoying the view from behind.

The captain fell into his new role. "Did I do it right?"

"You did good. You can fuck me tonight."

The captain pleaded, "Will you join me at my table for dinner?"

"I'm OS, a cadet. If I join you in the open, I'll lose respect from my comrades."

"Your comrades know your ass is mine. Respect isn't on the table any more."

Paxton smacked the captain hard. A smile spread across the older man's face. "Do it again."

15

MAKING THE ROUNDS

To maintain the social balance, Paxton stopped spending nights with the captain in his cuddy. As their ship, fully laden with cargo, rocketed towards its next waystation of Fortaleza, Paxton did the rounds, pleasing each sailor the way he best knew how. Trip got a regular mid-day blowjob. They met in the toilet. If it was busy, they waited until they could at least get started by themselves. Everyone knew Trip and many experienced the odd sensation of his loose floppy cock tripling in size in their mouths. If a sailor stumbled in on them while they were busy, he just stepped around them. After lunch, Rocky waited in his room for the handsome lad to come play Daddy and Son. After dinner, Paxton made a quick trip to see George, who always needed the relief. Later at night, he joined the captain for a colon-stretching session. He topped it all off with a light dessert: Brick. He could hardly feel Brick after the captain, but he always knew when his loose hole had brought the redhead to climax. Thick rivulets ran down his leg. All this work was outside of his normal job, and exhaustion set in. The captain ordered him to the ship's medic. There, he was given an unusual exam involving manual insertion into his rectal cavity.

"I already told you, Doc, I've been giving it away day and night. You'll find plenty of signs of wear and tear."

The doctor shone a flashlight through the back of his hospital gown and down his hole. "Son, you're fine. You just aren't getting enough sleep. You need a day or two to catch up on sleep. The captain requested you use his cuddy for privacy."

A knot of dread formed in Pax's stomach. He wouldn't get any rest at all.

"Listen, Doc, is there a bed up here in Sick Bay?"

"Well yes, it's not very comfortable."

"Can you tell the captain I need a couple days in isolation to be sure I ain't got the Dengue Fever?"

The middle-aged medic mopped his brow. "Son, it will be a terrible temptation having you here with me."

Paxton looked at the man's trousers. Nothing special. "Give in to temptation if you must."

The doctor was very gentle. He had studied surgery. His delicate touch was a new sensation for Paxton. He was used to being needed so bad that the caresses became greedy and strong. Not so with the medic. He lightly touched all the beautiful places on the young sailor. His hand brushed his nipples so softly, Paxton thought he'd dreamed it.

The doctor kissed Paxton like a butterfly landing on a magnolia blossom.

The fucking was gentle, too. The doctor was big, but not extremely so. He entered Paxton with mechanical precision. When he came, it was restrained. The doctor inhaled, held it, then let go softly, throbbing inside Paxton, coating him with a soft spray of semen. More butterfly kisses and it was over.

"Will you tell the captain I'm sick?"

"Yes."

"But do it in a way where he doesn't suspect anything."

"He's a suspicious man. But, okay."

For two glorious days, Paxton slept. He was interrupted occasionally by the doctor, but nobody got to visit because of the fear of contagion. It was brilliant. The doc was a vacation from extremes. He was neither tiny nor tremendous. He was Goldilocks sized. The doctor justified his rutting sessions as "treatments." To that end, he coated his prick with a homemade jelly containing cocaine and mercurochrome. It eased the burning, and helped the torn areas repair themselves. He wished the vacation could have lasted for weeks, but they were about to arrive in Fortaleza. The doctor sent him home with a medicine chest of remedies: oral morphine for pain, cod oil suppositories, and a whole tin of Amyl Nitrite.

16

ON THE TOWN

Brick walked in while he was putting away the stash.

"Morphine? Man!"

"You want some?" Paxton held up the bottle.

"You first," Brick insisted.

The cadet poured out a capful and swallowed it, nearly choking on the nasty flavor. "Oh, that's vile!"

"Just wait." Brick took a capful, and an extra swig.

It would be hard to say when the medicine blasted its way through their consciousness, but they were definitely still at sea when it started. Several horn blasts signaled their arrival. Fortaleza was a city of over half a million. It was the closest port to the Amazon, and all the trucks brought goods from up and down the river. American Cotton was in high demand, so that was the first to be unloaded. Here the stevedores were short and muscled. They whistled appreciation for Paxton's naturally tall, slender body. He blushed and smiled, which only made them chase him more. One charmer used his best English. He held Paxton's elbow.

"You come see the warehouse?" His accent was funny, like he was talking through his nose.

"I don't know. What's in the warehouse?"

The short, handsome man reached down and tugged on his bulky meat. "I'm Mateus."

"I'm Paxton and I'm stoned out of my mind on morphine!" He laughed, but Mateus only smiled. He didn't get it.

Before long, they were in a warehouse full of liquor, rubber, coffee and Brazil nuts. Mateus was strong. He lifted Paxton onto a sack of coffee beans, and held his legs aloft. He planted his mouth on Paxton's hole, slurping and licking with gusto. Mateus was not gentle. He was rough and strong. When he had slicked up Paxton's ass, he pulled out a billy club of a cock. It wasn't as long as Rocky, but it was thicker than the captain. It was the size and shape of a can of Bohemia. Mateus expected the usual cries of protest, but Paxton welcomed him inside with ease. The morphine made it easy to ignore the ripping flesh. There was blood, but it didn't hurt. Mateus paused.

"Is okay?"

"Fuck me." Paxton surprised the Brazilian muscle man. He pulled hard, forcing Mateus inside him until his balls smacked his butt cheeks.

"Porra!" Mateus was astonished. Never had a man or woman taken all of him so quickly and easily.

"Damn you're so fucking thick!" Paxton threw his head back, moaning with delight. "Fuck me!"

Mateus had powerful thighs. He pumped his meat forcefully into the young sailor. Paxton writhed and squirmed at the assault on his anus.

Mateus held Paxton down by pressing on his belly. He ravaged the hole until it was stretched and sloppy.

Paxton couldn't ejaculate on Morphine, but he could come like a woman. His body shook with anal orgasm.

"Ooooooohhhh!" Paxton's holler reverberated through the empty warehouse. Mateus continued his assault on Paxton's ass. The sailor's anal orgasms caused tight spasms that massaged the stevedore's thick meat.

"Unnnh!" Mateus was close. "I come."

"Inside me. Fill me up."

Mateus didn't speak a lot of English, but he understood that command. In giant spurts, he emptied his balls into the American sailor.

Paxton leaned in to kiss the stevedore, but he pulled away. With a violent popping sound, the barrel-chested Brazilian yanked his chunky cock out of the boy's ass, leaving webs of come in its wake. The coffee bags were slick with spit and come.

With his powerful arms, Mateus lifted Paxton to his feet.

"Thank you for I fuck you."

His awkward English was charming.

"You're welcome." He tried to kiss his Brazilian companion, but Mateus pulled away.

"I kiss only women. But you are, eh, a maravilhoso ass."

Mateus was a wonderful introduction to Fortaleza. He was able to explain in broken English that the name Fortaleza means fortress, but also strength. Pax squeezed the stevedore's giant arm and smiled. "They weren't kidding."

Mateus had to get back to his wife and kids. His shift had been over for at least an hour; they would worry.

"Is Fortaleza dangerous?"

"It is most dangerous city in all of Brazil. Stay by docks; you are safe."

How dangerous could such a beautiful city really be? Pax was still reeling from the morphine, and he yearned to shake off his legs and see something other than a grey metal wall full of rivets. "Mateus, can I walk with you towards town?"

"Yes, but take ka-hoo back to ship."

"Ka-hoo, okay."

On land, the attention of men is not always directed

towards potential partners. Strong, handsome men paid no attention to Paxton's graceful body. A few did notice him walking the strand with the handsome stevedore; they kept their distance. Mateus looked like he could tear them in two.

"If they only knew how gentle he is," Paxton thought to himself.

The beach ended at a plaza with several towers and fortresses. Mateus pointed towards the colorful plaza.

"Heart of the city."

"Will you stay?" There were far more suspicious people lurking than Paxton had imagined.

Mateus pointed to his wrist and shook his head.

"Malandros." He gestured at the sprinkling of thugs that peppered the square. "Policia, en nenhuma parte. Dangerous."

Paxton still had twelve hours to enjoy dry land. He was not going to let these ne'er-do-wells ruin his shore leave. Just before Mateus parted ways, he pointed to a saloon called "Curzon." Pax thanked the man, who said "Oh-bray-god-do" back to him.

17

THE CURZON

The contrast between the equatorial sunlight and the dark bar left Paxton temporarily blind upon first entering. The bartender, who was polishing a table, vaulted over the bar like an Olympian. The place was empty.

"Sorry, sir, It's a bit early still." He was British, with light brown hair and matching eyes. Paxton was a sucker for an English accent.

"What part of the Kingdom are you from?" he asked.

"Derby. Little city, not much happening." The bartender did a backflip behind the bar. "What can I get you?"

Paxton was still numb from morphine. He examined at the bartender's hands.

"You're not married?"

The man blushed. "Do you know what sort of place this is?"

"I do now." Paxton sat facing him. "I'll have your local special."

"Caipirinha." The bartender grabbed some rather dusty supplies.

"What's that?"

"Cachaça, sugar and lime." He poured a clear tonic

over the sugar cubes, then squeezed a lime and sprinkled some powdered sugar into the cocktail. "Taste it."

Paxton had a few sips, then downed a big swig. "This is incredible."

"Thanks. May I ask, the way you're dressed, are you a sailor?"

"I'm OS - an ordinary seaman."

The bartender grinned. "You're American, but from where? I don't know the accent."

"N'Awlins," Pax exaggerated the accent, to the delight of his new admirer.

"I'm Donald, by the way." He extended a well-manicured hand.

"Paxton Smalls, at your service." He saluted. The morphine and drink were a powerful combination.

"At my service, he says? Do you have a menu?" He topped off Paxton's glass.

Paxton sized up Donald. He remembered his gymnast's leaps over the bar. He checked below his waist. Nothing remarkable stood out, but it was hard to tell with linen.

Donald lifted the hinged countertop. Paxton joined him behind the bar.

While the sailor greedily explored the sinewy curves hidden under linen, Donald focused intensely on Paxton's best asset. The barman put his hand down the back of hiss dungarees, inserted his finger into the loose hole, and held it to his nose. He sniffed the perfume, then put it in his mouth. "Fresh come. You've been busy."

Paxton roved along the tight muscles, making his way eventually to the thighs. Nothing hung down - Donald was not one of the big boys. But Paxton found a decent cock standing at attention under the summer fabric. He rubbed it a few times. It was not going to do much damage.

"What time do you get off? Paxton asked.

"Right now." The barman guided him to his knees. "You're young. Do you know how to—"

He couldn't finish his sentence before Paxton had swallowed his entire cock.

Donald was a nimble gymnast. He stood on the second shelf and used his arms to push up from the bar. He plunged into Paxton's greedy mouth.

The effects of the Caipirinha were strong enough to melt the walls. The young sailor stood up and steadied himself against the bar.

"What did you put in my—?" But Paxton never finished his sentence. After a crushing blow to the back of his head, he watched the floor rise up to meet his chin.

Paxton woke up to Brick and Rocky carrying him by his arms and legs along the Praia Iracema towards the docks at Mucuripe.

"What's going on?"

"You got mugged."

"Is Donald okay? Was he hurt?"

"Who?"

"Donald, the bartender."

"Curzon has been closed for years. There's no bartender, Pax." Rocky set him on a park bench.

"Then, who was that?"

"Probably the man who stole your wallet. Did he get your passport?"

Paxton kept that in his underwear, next to his small parts, because no man ever went there. It was still there. He held it aloft.

"That would have been a real problem," Brick said. "How much did he get?"

"Not much. I left most of my money in — well where I leave it."

Rocky held his chin. "You don't know how lucky you are. Brazil is a dangerous place, and Fortaleza is the most dangerous of all the cities."

"More than Sao Paulo?"

"It's the docks. It's just a rough town. How's your head. Is it bleeding?"

It was. But Paxton felt fine. The morphine was a long, steady cushion between all types of pain.

"I just need a little morphine; I'll be right as rain."

"Morphine?" The Third Officer was annoyed.

"Yeah…the captain is, well, he does a lot of damage."

Brick stayed quiet. He was high on the same stuff, and didn't need Rocky sanctioning him.

"I wonder why Mateus directed me to Curzon. Wouldn't he know it was closed?"

"My guess he was part of the con," Rocky reasoned.

Brick cleared his throat. "Let's get a carro."

"Mateus said to get a Ka-hoo."

"Brick chuckled. Same thing. That's how they say it in Brazil."

A carro turned out to be a horse and carriage, fighting its way through modern traffic. The carrro cost a fraction of a taxicab. Unlike taxi drivers, the carro driver was trustworthy and kind.

Paxton's head was a bruised watermelon by the time he boarded ship. He took two capfuls of Morphine and drifted off to sleep.

❧ 18 ❧

THE CAPTAIN'S FIB

When Paxton regained consciousness, he was In the cuddy. The morphine could no longer protect him from the pain that encircled his skull.

The captain appeared in his foggy field of vision. He smiled like a priest might smile at a choirboy. "You have a lump on the back of your head. It's bigger than your dick."

Paxton groaned. "That doesn't sound too serious."

"You could fuck someone with it." There was a bead of sweat trickling down his brow.

"Why am I in your cuddy and not the hospital?"

"I prefer our doctor. He's more...familiar with the way a merchant marine operates."

"When will he be here?"

"He came already, you don't remember?"

Paxton shook his head and winced.

"He said to keep an eye on you for signs of brain swelling. Brick's got the first watch."

The captain closed the door on his way out. Brick leaned forward into Paxton's field of vision. "Hey, Kid. Feeling better?"

"Better than what?"

"Better than last night."

Paxton shook his head, slowly this time. "I got mugged, right?"

Brick nodded. "We got you back in one piece. You'll be sore for a while, but you'll make it."

"Why didn't the doctor wake me up?"

Brick frowned. "There was no doctor, I'm afraid."

"Why not?"

"The medic would have sent you to the hospital, then the captain might have lost his rank over this. One look at your stretched asshole and the hospital could file charges against anyone you named."

"It ain't illegal in Brazil."

"Maritime law is complicated."

Paxton frowned. "I would never give anyone up."

"With what the captain's packing, he'd be the prime suspect."

"I don't get why it's even a crime."

Brick smiled. "It boils down to some lines in the Bible that lawmakers cling to out of all proportion to others. I don't know why."

It was near sunset. "How long have I been out? It's nearly dark."

"You slept a long time, Pax."

"I'm starved. You got something to eat?"

Brick produced a covered bowl from the captain's desk.

"George brought this for you about an hour ago. It's still warm."

Paxton lifted the cover and was greeted by a tantalizing aroma. It was a blend of onions, greens, garlic, and an oily chicken broth. As he dipped cornbread into the stew, he discovered thick slices of sausage. With each bite, Paxton's strength returned. It hurt his ribs to raise the spoon. It didn't matter; the soup's savory goodness outweighed his bodily pain.

Brick leaned over and whispered, "The captain is

just making sure you're well enough for him to fuck. He can't wait a fucking day."

Paxton propped himself on his elbows. "How will he know when I'm ready?"

"He's asked me to warm you up."

Paxton guffawed. "That's the difference between a spoon and a shovel! No offense, Brick."

"No, you're right. He's half crazed over you. I'll just tell him you weren't ready."

"But Brick, tonight could be our last night together before Rio. I want you to fuck me,"

Brick gently pulled the young man by the legs, draping them over his freckled shoulders. He wiped spit and petroleum jelly on the perfect asshole.

Paxton grinned. "Fuck me."

Brick's small cock entered him effortlessly. They each exhaled a loud sigh. Brick was not big, but he had a magnificent technique that no big cock could ever hope to rival. He stayed pressed against the boy's backside so as not to fall out. He shoved and jammed his way into Paxton's rectum, pressing against his Cowper's glands. A clear, steady stream of sticky fluid oozed from Paxton's tiny penis.

The younger sailor moaned. Tears streamed down his cheeks.

Brick stopped short, "Am I hurting you? God, I'm sorry."

Paxton shook his head. "It's not that, Brick. You made me love you, and soon you'll be gone. Who will protect me?"

Brick intensified his powerful thrusts. "Don't worry kid, Rocky's got your back. And if Erasmus replaces me, he'll protect you to the death on my mere say-so." Never losing a beat, he wiped the tears from his bunk-mate's face. It didn't work. They returned in a downpour.

Paxton knew his tears would make Brick soft, but he couldn't control them.

"Kid, I had no idea you were so sweet on me. It almost makes me wish I'd never met my wife and had those kids."

"Leave her."

Brick stopped thrusting abruptly. "That isn't funny."

"It's not supposed to be."

Brick pulled out. "I'll tell the captain you're still too banged up for sex."

"No! Brick, wait!" He left the cuddy. Paxton was alone with his thoughts. They were bad and his emotions were worse. The huge lump on the back of his head throbbed. Carefully, he got to his feet and rifled through the captain's dresser. In the sock drawer he found five bottles of morphine tablets. He took three tablets from each bottle before returning it to the drawer. He swallowed two and washed them down with a glass of scotch.

Within ten minutes, the effects of the scotch grew stronger, and then the pain relief kicked in. Sad, lonely, and high, Paxton drifted off to sleep.

19

MAKE-UP SEX

The next morning Paxton popped two pills and joined the crew at breakfast.

He was astonished at how happy they were to see him. The men were careful not to hug him or clap them on the back. They touched his shoulder or patted his rump. The gentle hands brushing his skin in combination with morphine was enough to send him into bliss. They could never tell, but he had an erection under his white sailor pants. A spot formed, giving him away. He was careful to keep his hand hitched to his pocket to cover the wet stain.

Trip brought Paxton a tray of breakfast. George had slipped in some Portuguese sausage to make the meal special.

Brick was the only sailor sitting out the little welcome party. He ate in the corner of the mess. As soon as Paxton could break away he went to the room. Brick was moping on the bottom bunk.

"Hey," Paxton tested the waters.

Brick heaved a sigh. "Hi."

"I'm sorry about what I said. I know your family means the world to you. I'm just a friend."

Brick grunted. His frown remained.

"Even though you have more important people to

care for, I need you to know how important you've been to me. You taught me how to get fucked. You made me come for the first time in my life. You showed me who and what I am, for Christ's sake."

Brick looked up. "And?"

"And I don't want our last day together to be a piece of shit."

Brick's lips curled into a smile. "How do you propose to turn it around?"

"Since you're already on my bed, scoot over."

Paxton lowered his pants and lay on his side. Brick whistled.

"Your ass gets me hard just looking at it." He spit into his cupped hand. He wiped Paxton's hole to make it slick. In seconds, he was inside thrusting his rock hard cock in and out in a slow, steady rhythm. He planted his lips on the boy's neckline and sucked his skin, leaving little welts. His freckled skin glistened with sweat. The morning had just begun, but the temperature soared.

Brick reached one arm around and held Paxton's teat between his thumb and forefinger. On each inward thrust he pinched hard, releasing on the out stroke. His perfect little penis pressed in all the right places. Paxton moaned in soft assent. Brick reached between the sailor's legs and found the tiny mound of flesh there. He massaged it. Paxton's moans became howls. He greedily devoured his three course meal of ass, nipple, and genital stimulation.

For dessert, Brick ran his stubble along the skin where the neck meets the shoulder, kissing it in tiny droplets. Spasms of pleasure caused Paxton to writhe and kick. His writhing in turn caused the redhead's cock to swell further.

The spasms grew more frequent, as Paxton built toward a full body orgasm. Brick was big and powerful when stroking Paxton's tiny penis. It gushed clear pre-come all over his hand. He put it to his lips and sniffed before tasting. It smelled like pussy juice. He greedily gulped it down.

Paxton couldn't stay quiet. The seizures that spread deep, intense pleasure from the knot on his head to his pinky toe grew more powerful.

"Yes! Yes! Oh! Yes!" All the noise was bound to attract attention.

Brick's breath grew shallow and rapid. When he had licked the fingers clean he put his hand between Paxton's legs again. Paxton stared over his shoulder at his roommate; their eyes locked. Silently, each let the other know it was time.

Brick planted his lips on Paxton's, pressing his tongue deep. He swabbed the back of the lad's throat. If he could force it deeper he would have. Their eyes closed. A strong love washed over them, different from love of family or brothers. It was the love of a dear friend whom you knew you might never see again. Their love was the sensation that overturned the bucket. Paxton's tiny penis shot a long white rope that flew between Brick's fingers to splatter on the wall opposite. He rubbed gently to coax out more and more come in warm, wet missiles.

Brick was churning up a warm salty brew of his own. When Paxton shot like a tiny gun and spasmed against his hips and belly, it brought the redhead to orgasm. He panted, releasing a flood of semen. The sphincter muscles, not yet destroyed by the captain, became a hand milking an udder. Each contraction caused him to dump another gob of semen inside Paxton. Despite there being plenty of spare room inside the rectum, Brick's sperm overflowed and sprayed out the hole and onto his freckled belly in violent spurts. It took nine pulses before his balls were drained of ejaculate.

The two men held each other lovingly, spoon fashion. Paxton wished it would last a lifetime, but it was only a matter of three or four seconds before their union was shattered by a loud clapping. The captain stood in the doorway, his monstrous cock throbbing down his right leg.

"Bravo, gentlemen. Color me impressed."

Paxton froze. Was he in trouble? Worse, was Brick in trouble? His head flooded with dozens of horrible outcomes. He chose to save Brick.

"I'm ready now, sir." He turned to Brick. "Thanks, man. I needed a warm-up before he tears me in two with that monster."

The captain rubbed his right thigh and chuckled. "Good work, Brick. Now grab a holystone and scrub the poop deck. I need this young man's hole."

Brick gave a smile that contained a thousand words. He was grateful for Paxton's quick thinking and sacrifice. He was going to miss Paxton. The sex was great. It would never happen again. This was goodbye.

Brick saluted and left the room.

20

THE CUDDY SLAVE

The captain grinned. "You ready for this?" He grabbed the log of flesh for emphasis. He escorted Paxton back to the makeshift sex prison called the cuddy.

Paxton was trapped. He dropped his trousers and presented his dripping hole.

The captain was gentle. He knew Paxton had many bruises and bumps. He was greedy and lustful, but he wasn't a devil. He kissed and licked his exposed asshole, then stood.

"You're not to leave this room unless I say so."

To emphasize his point, he turned the key in the lock and put it in his pocket.

"But Sir, how will I get out if the ship is sinking?"

"Do you think I'm such a bad captain that I'll sink this ship?"

Paxton shook his head.

"Good. Because I have a big ship that hasn't docked in days. I'm going to open the port."

He produced a tub of Albolene and with a wave of his hand, commanded Paxton to spread it on his hole.

Images and desires collided in Paxton's head. The captain's cock was the thickest, if not quite the longest he had ever seen. But it was rock hard. It was like being fucked by a wine bottle. There was no give. He could fill his rectum, but he couldn't go where George had been, so the secret room remained empty. The captain was strong, powerful, and virile. He made Paxton feel like a little girl. But the captain's kisses tasted strange. He was much older, perhaps more than twice Paxton's age. He earned a lot of money. If he brought Paxton ashore, he would spoil him with expensive gifts and fancy meals. Paxton should love this handsome man and lust for his huge insatiable cock, but he didn't. 'It's something I could get used to,' he told himself. Having known love or a close facsimile with Brick, he knew he was lying to himself. The captain was not a man he could ever love. And now he was locked in the cuddy, a concubine or worse.

"Hey! Where did you go?"

Paxton saluted. The captain chuckled.

"At ease, sailor. I need you nice and relaxed."

The captain unbuckled his white trousers and pushed them towards his knees. His hard cock made it difficult.

"Can I get a hand here?"

The captain put his hands on his hips while Paxton struggled to work the massive cock out of the pant leg. When at last he set it free, the cock sprang up and clipped Paxton's chin.

"Suck it."

"I beg your pardon?"

"You heard me. Do your best. Just lick the tip if that's all you can handle."

Paxton was turned on in spite of himself. The captain's gravity defying cock pointed skyward above Paxton's Head. It already leaked pre-come from the tip. The size and stony hardness proved there was art in nature. It was a carved statue in flesh. The solid head peeked out of the soft foreskin. Paxton raised from a sitting to a standing kneel to reach the zenith.

He licked the salty head and worked his tongue under the foreskin, circling the colossal head in wide strokes. He wrapped one arm around the log of flesh to steady himself.

"Can you suck it?" The captain sounded like a child whining for a corn dog at the carnival.

Paxton clamped his mouth over the top of the head. It was comical, like a lamprey clamped to a much bigger fish.

The captain, careful to avoid the swollen bump, pressed hard on Paxton's head, forcing more and more of his cock into his mouth. The stretch was so severe, he the corners of his mouth tore. He wrapped his lips over his teeth to keep the cock from getting scraped up.

Suddenly, the captain bucked his hips forward, burying himself deep. The cockhead tore its way past Paxton's tonsils and landed deep in his esophagus. The older man sighed with contentment, but Paxton couldn't breathe. He coughed and retched until the cock and a load of clear thick saliva forced its way out of his mouth. The captain caught it in his palm and rubbed it on his cock.

"I juiced you. Now it'll be smooth. Ready for more?"

Paxton nodded. The goopy saliva acted as a lubricant, allowing the captain to slide in and out of Paxton's throat with ease. Paxton's eyes watered. The salty tears burned the wounds on the corners of his mouth. It was impossible to keep from retching. Each time he retched, the captain smacked him on the cheek.

"No more of that now. You love my big cock in your mouth, don't you?"

Paxton nodded.

"Say it." He pulled out.

"I love your big cock in my mouth." Paxton's larynx was bruised, so the words came out in a hoarse whisper.

He plunged past the tonsils again and remained there, choking him.

"Do you want it in your ass?"

Paxton was ashamed how badly he wanted it. He nodded, and the captain pulled out, his cock covered in curtains of thick saliva.

"Let me see your hole."

Paxton presented his hole to the captain like a cat in heat. Anything to keep it out of his mouth. His throat was on fire worse than the time he got mumps.

"Spread it."

Paxton held his cheeks apart to show off his asshole. Brick's semen oozed out, dripping down his balls.

The captain snorted, "Is that your roommate's pecker juice?"

"Yes, sir."

"Good. Between that, the Albolene, and your throat spit, we're gonna have a smooth ride."

It was smooth. Paxton was relieved when the massive meat slid easily into his ass. Nothing tore, and he could breathe. He was used to the captain's hardness and girth. He even liked the way he kept hitting the back of his rectum. He looked over his shoulder and saw the captain playing with his own teats. He twisted them. They sprouted gray hairs.

"You have such a pretty face. Lie on your back for me will you?"

Paxton rotated, skewered by the captain, until they faced each other. The old man hunched over and pressed his cigar stained mustache to Paxton's lips in a one-way passionate kiss.

Paxton took his tongue into his mouth and let him lick his teeth and the roof of his mouth. After his kiss with Brick, it was empty. But he pretended to like it.

The captain pulled his cock out and pushed Paxton's cheeks apart. The girth made his hole stay open like a wishing well. He blew air in it. Paxton writhed in ecstasy. He plugged it back up with his giant cork and fucked hard. Paxton's head hit the wall a few times before the captain realized what he was doing.

Paxton didn't care. He had crossed an invisible hurdle, loving the sensation of being filled and stretched. Sex was good, no matter how he felt about the guy fucking him. He needed the captain to fill him with his come. He reached up like an infant reaching for his mother until his hands clamped over the old man's nipples. He twisted them hard.

"You're gonna make me come!"

"That's the idea, isn't it?"

"I wanna come down your throat."

Paxton smiled to cover his fear and disappointment.

The captain pulled out and rammed his ass-stained cock down Paxton's throat. In this position, he was pinned to the bed, a butterfly on a spreading board. He couldn't stop the captain from choking him. Luckily, the old man knew how to fuck a throat. Paxton coughed up sputum so hard, it flew out his nose. He tasted his own ass, which made him retch again. But soon, the captain was sliding in and out of Paxton's throat without a cough or retch. Paxton accepted the captain all the way, so his pubic hairs were smashed against his nose. He stayed there, taking little short strokes, softly growling.

Paxton couldn't breathe, but that only made him more excited. His throat belonged to the captain. He reached up and twisted the captain's nipples.

"Oh shit!" The captain staggered backwards, giving Paxton a chance to breathe before the captain leaned in and started pounding furiously. Paxton didn't enjoy his throat stretched and filled. He preferred to have his ass stuffed. But his mouth being used as a fuckhole was exciting. The captain controlled everything: his breath, the depth he plowed, the place he would leave his sperm.

"Get ready!"

Paxton coughed as the first load landed deep in his throat. By the time the second burst erupted, the massive cock was pointed at Paxton's mouth. It had been a couple of days and the captain was full of built up semen. That second burst landed in a huge splash across Paxton's face. He swallowed and licked what he could as two more pumps came. Then the captain went all the way to the balls down his throat and fired several more nourishing bullets of semen before withdrawing. He collapsed beside Paxton, out of breath.

"You're my prisoner now; remember that."

"Yes, sir." Paxton felt his control over the Captain slip away. He was locked in a gilded cage.

And he remained a prisoner until they got to Rio, where everything changed.

21

THEY GOT A LOT OF
COFFEE IN BRAZIL

As the ship pulled into Guanabara Bay, Paxton churned with inner conflict. Pain, both physical and emotional, clouded his thoughts. His head throbbed. The captain had nearly split him in two, then tore through his tonsils. It hurt to swallow. His heart fared no better. Brick was leaving him in the hands of the captain, and a stranger was taking his bunk. Even if that stranger turned out to be Brick's buddy Erasmus, there was a whole layer cake of emotions Paxton couldn't shake: fear, loss, betrayal, hope and above all - sadness. He was a prisoner in the captain's cuddy. No, more than a prisoner, a sex slave. Paxton's tiny member matched the size of his self-esteem. He preferred being paid attention, even if it was for painful sex. He was worthless, and deserved to be fucked bloody every night by the slave master he called captain.

The horn gave one short blast, indicating the ship was changing course to the port side. Paxton stood on his knees to gaze out of the tiny porthole in his sex prison. As the boat came around port side, Paxton marveled at the city. It made New Orleans look like a ghost town. Rio was comprised of thousands of high rise apartment buildings at sea level. They were flanked with colorful gardens and trees bearing flowers in bright colors Paxton had never seen. The hillsides were covered with ramshackle houses. Over the whole city presided the Natural wonder of Sugarloaf and the man-made beauty of the enormous Christ the Redeemer on Corcovado. He had seen black and white pictures in the atlas. Even back then when they were taken, the city was impressive. Now, ten years later, in vibrant color, it was a kaleidoscope of scenery. New Orleans had a dozen high rises in the Faubourg Ste. Marie. To see thousands in neat rows beside each other was astonishing.

The captain surprised him from behind. He put a meaty paw on Paxton's rump and squeezed.

"It gets bigger every day."

Paxton was unsure if he meant Rio or his throbbing cock that strained against his pantleg.

"It's breathtaking."

"I'll tell you what, Paxton. If you promise to keep out of trouble, I'll let you go exploring. I can't have a repeat of what happened to you in Fortaleza. But first, I have something that needs your attention."

Paxton didn't turn around. He groaned inwardly when he heard the belt loosening and the fly come unbuttoned. The captain's pants dropped around his ankles, releasing the foot-long summer sausage.

Powerless to prevent what came next, Paxton surrendered. Silently, he lowered his dungarees, exposing his perfect round rump and tiny genitals. The captain buried his face in Paxton's bumhole, loosening it with his tongue. Paxton moaned with pleasure, despite his misgivings. The captain was an ace in the art of eating ass. Paxton's legs trembled. The captain held him by the waist and dug his tongue in deep.

"Oh God. Don't. Stop. Don't. Stop." Paxton couldn't resist the captain's artful tongue. He was a salt-lick for the horse of a man buried nose deep in his crack. Paxton spread his cheeks, allowing the captain more surface area to work his magic. The older man gently tweaked Paxton's nipples. The young lad dribbled his clear syrup on the floor. He was no further in his career than his mother. He was a whore. The only way to get through the captain's frequent penetrations was to surrender completely. The more he focused on the joy of being stuffed beyond capacity with cock, the easier his work became. He knew his mother must do the same.

Behind him, he could hear the captain uncap a tub of Vaseline. The sound he made greasing his bloated cock sounded like a cat lapping up a bowl of milk. The rough fingers pried at his hole. He was stretched and loose from all he had endured on the seas in the past two weeks. His anus no longer puckered. It hung in a wrinkled pout, like a vagina.

He tuned out all pain and inhaled the captain into his hole. In spite of everything, he still loved when the old man fucked him. There were sharp jabs of pain, ripping sensations, things coming loose that shouldn't; Paxton focused on the fullness and it all quieted. The captain tried hard to be a good lover. He held Paxton by the waist while he destroyed his sphincter, and showered him with kisses. Paxton turned his head to kiss back. The captain believed he was the world's greatest lover hearing the lad's cries of "Oh yes! Oh right there!" It was his job now. He'd heard his mother do it a thousand times. It sped things along.

The captain was crotch deep inside Paxton, pounding mercilessly at the rectum wall past which he was too fat and hard to navigate. With blunt force, the officer tore and pounded at his ass, caring very little if it hurt or even killed him. Paxton moaned and shouted false encouragement until, like happens with sex, he believed himself. He talked his way into enjoying this anal pillaging. It was the stuffed sensation, the rhythmic thrusts, and the big smile combined with the beads of sweat falling from the captain's brow onto Paxton's back that heralded the stirrings of orgasm in his belly.

He tossed all resentments and fears aside. He focused on making the captain happier and happier. He played with the old man's teats, pinching the nipples hard. In response, Paxton felt him shudder, sending waves of electric pleasure between them as the rhythm was interrupted by the shaking. He reached back and cupped the captain's balls, gently squeezing them as if he could wring out come from there. It made the passageway much slipperier as the captain leaked a slick trail of pre-come.

"Oh Paxton, you beautiful boy. I can't believe how easy it was to break you in."

Paxton stared out the porthole. He ignored the comparison to a pair of shoes.

He moaned as he uttered a few words. "Ohhh. Fuck. You feel so good inside me."

It was true, even if Paxton didn't want it to be. He had brought himself to the precipice of orgasm with lies that became the truth.

"Shit! Oh shit!" Paxton rounded his lips and gave a surprised grunt as his tiny penis shot semen all over the wall in front of him.

"Did I do that? You didn't even use your hands!" The captain was astonished.

"You fucked it out of me, sir. And it's coming again." Another wave of orgasm washed over the boy as he sprayed another heavy load of sperm across the wall.

It must have been a huge turn on for the captain, because he made low grunting sounds, a pig in a trough, and bucked to a completely new beat. He unloaded enough semen to impregnate ten women. His cock grew soft like an elephant's trunk, then slipped out of

Paxton's loose cunt. Paxton shivered with joy and disgust as he shat out the captain's tool.

The captain left the cuddy door unlocked. Paxton found an envelope bearing his name; it contained 10 five dollar bills.

22

GREEN CARNATION,
BLUE EYES

Paxton ran to his room to see if Brick was there, but someone new was already in the top bunk, with his back to Paxton as he tucked in the sheets.

Before he saw anything else, Paxton saw the green carnation tattooed on his forearm. The new roommate turned to face him. He had the same deep blue eyes he remembered from the wharf that awful wonderful day six months ago. His smile lit up the room.

"You must be Paxton. Brick told me all about you. Hey, I know you! New Orleans." He remembered Paxton, too.

Paxton blushed. "Uh yeah, I remember."

"I jacked off for two weeks just picturing your little ass."

Now Paxton was crimson.

"Oh don't worry, I won't try and fuck you. I can't. It's not physically possible." He rubbed the tip of his serpentine cock where it rested just below his knee. "A man can dream, though, right?"

Paxton nodded. He smelled that faint spiced rum cologne and the whole love at first sight sensation came rushing back, making him swoon. He held onto the ladder for support.

"Have you been to Rio before?"

Paxton shook his head. The cat had his tongue for sure.

"Well then, let's go see the sights, Paxton. Oh, how rude of me. I'm Erasmus."

The waterfront was alive with nightclubs, restaurants, bars and dance halls. Erasmus led the way as the two sailors strutted down Atlantic Avenue. Women and men alike turned their heads for a second glance at Paxton's face. A few eyes wandered further down and widened at the anaconda in Erasmus's trousers.

The young sailor relied on his new friend to guide him.

"Up this street, there's the best feijoada in Rio." Erasmus pointed up a narrow side street.

"What's feijoada?"

"Are you hungry?"

Paxton nodded. He was starving.

"Then you're about to find out."

Feijoada turned out to be a rich stew made with beans and sausages. It was like Red Beans and Rice times ten. The restaurant brought endless baskets of 'pao de queijo' - little biscuits made with a white melty cheese. They dipped the biscuits in the stew and it was like heaven.

"Brick tells me you and he made it together."

Paxton nearly choked on his stew. "What else did he tell you?"

"He told me you got a nasty knock on the head, and ever since, you've been in love with the captain."

"I'm not in love with him. I was in love with Brick, but he had a family. The captain can have me fired, so I gotta act like I'm into him."

Erasmus pounded the table so hard he nearly split the wood in two. "Not again. That bastard."

Paxton had questions, but a dessert of little balls of chocolate called Brigadeiro arrived at the table, and they both forgot everything. There was one ball left. Paxton eyed it hungrily, but Erasmus snatched it from the plate. He waited for Paxton's frown, then reached across and pressed the savory ball into the boy's mouth.

Erasmus brushed Paxtons lips with his manly thumb as he withdrew. Paxton longed to hold on to it and suck it. He shook his head. He was the captain's property now. This night out was all the freedom he would get.

"You know, when I saw you that first day on the wharf, I decided to become a Merchant Marine."

Erasmus chuckled. "Those guys were teasing you mercilessly. Why on Earth did you decide to join them?"

"It was you more than anything. You were so kind and protective."

Erasmus shrugged. Paxton worried he may have said too much.

"And it was the way that all of you were like a family. I never had that."

"Are your folks okay with you being a Merchant Marine?"

"I don't know my Dad. My mom misses me, but she's proud."

"It's a good gig, so long as there's peace. If we get another big war, you will regret it. Ask the captain, he can tell you what it was like running cargo in the Atlantic during the war."

"Erasmus, I don't want to talk to the captain. I like talking to you."

Erasmus cast him a worried glance. "Be careful with him."

"I am. I have him believing he's the best lover in the world."

"Brick says it's like being fucked with an oil derrick."

Paxton laughed. "Brick did it with the captain?"

Erasmus sighed. "He didn't have a choice. None of us do if he sets his sights on us."

Paxton frowned. "You too?"

Erasmus grabbed a waiter. "Duas Bohemias, por favor."

Paxton wanted to know. "Erasmus, did the captain...?"

"I heard you. I need a beer before I can talk about it."

❧ 23 ❧

SUGAR LOAF

The two roommates enjoyed the bitter brew. Erasmus ordered two more and then opened up.

"Paxton, everyone learns in the Merchant Marine how to get off with other men. If we didn't, we'd probably kill each other."

Paxton drained his bottle and nodded.

"And you know it's illegal, right?"

Paxton shook his head.

"Yeah, you can get court-martialed if the captain turns you in."

"But Captain Alder wouldn't do that, would he?"

"As long as we follow his orders, and do his bidding, we're safe."

"If he did that, wouldn't he get arrested too?"

Erasmus shrugged. "Maybe, but he's the C.O. It would be anyone's word against his."

Paxton took two bottles from the waiter and passed one to Erasmus.

Erasmus continued. "Captain Alder chooses which laws to enforce. As long as he gets a piece of ass every night, we're all safe. He likes the young, pretty ones best. I was young when I first joined his ship. The other guys broke me in the first couple of days, and then I went off to the captain's cabin. He was cruel with me, because I'm so much bigger than him. He likes his boys with small ones, like Brick...and you."

Paxton blushed crimson. He hated that his tiny penis was common knowledge.

"If you think the captain is rough with you, just imagine him taking out his rage on me. Every day my cock threatened his masculinity. But I let him have me. It's not like I could ever fuck someone with this." He grabbed his cock mid-thigh.

Paxton frowned. "You called it your 'Albatross.' What does that mean?"

"Coleridge."

Paxton shook his head. "I don't understand."

"It was an epic poem. 'The Rime of the Ancient Mariner.' The sailor kills an Albatross and the crew members make him wear the giant bird around his neck. It's a sailor's heavy curse."

"Well, my tiny hummingbird isn't much better." They clinked bottles in a toast.

Erasmus raised one eyebrow, a golden beer light shining through the misty blue. "It's the same curse, Paxton."

"I don't understand. From what I see, you have more than enough. I have nothing."

"Too much might as well be nothing. What did they call you in school? I got 'horseman', 'gate crasher', how about you?"

"Inchworm. Teeny Weenie."

They both sat in silent contemplation, nursing their beers.

Paxton spoke. "God is an asshole."

Erasmus laughed. "That's probably the only asshole I could ever fuck."

Paxton was giddy. "I'll bet I could take you."

Erasmus lost his smile. "No one can. Don't even joke about it."

"I'm serious."

Erasmus narrowed his eyes. "I like you kid. I would only hurt you. I know my cock looks like the grand prize, but it's not built for sex."

Paxton sighed. He could tell he was walking on landmines. "The captain would never let you near me, anyway."

"What do you mean? We share a room, kid."

Paxton shook his head. "He keeps me locked in the cuddy. I'm not allowed out. Someone brings me my meals."

Erasmus's jaw dropped. "That's not right, Pax. He's never done that before."

Paxton shrugged. "Lucky me. He fucks me morning, noon and night. I'm his slave."

"He's gone too far. We gotta get you out of there," Erasmus said.

"It's okay. I like getting fucked. He's not very good at it, not like Brick, but I still like it."

The two bottles of beer made their way through the two men quickly.

Together, they staggered to the banheiro.

Paxton unzipped and pulled his tiny penis out. Erasmus was a good guy. He wouldn't ridicule him. He turned and watched his roommate struggle to extract his never-ending hose of flesh from his pants leg. Paxton was done pissing before Erasmus finally freed the apple-sized head from his trousers. He had to take a step back to give himself enough space to piss without contact or splashback. Paxton absently played with himself, craving the frighteningly large cock Erasmus expertly aimed like a long rifle. Paxton put a hand on Erasmus's massive balls, rubbing them with fascination.

"Man, even your balls are huge."

Erasmus was done, and as he shook off the last droplets, the familiar flow of blood filled his cock, swelling it and lifting it away from his body.

He pushed Paxton's hand away. "Don't start evil."

The younger man licked his lips. "I'll bet I can get you off." He held Erasmus by the base of his cock, and stroked him. His fingers couldn't touch, and still the girth increased as more and more blood filled the massive chambers of the sailor's cock. It towered over the two men like Sugar Loaf over Rio.

Paxton stood behind Erasmus, stroking him. He closed his eyes and pretended it was his own. He spit in his palm to make the stroking easier. It dried quickly and he spit again. Erasmus arched his back and surrendered. His breath grew shallow. He let his head roll back onto the shoulder behind him.

"I get lightheaded, Pax. Don't let me pass out."

Paxton wrapped his free arm around the sailor's broad chest. "I got you, Raz."

The sailor's cock grew and grew. Paxton marveled that nature could have created something so absurdly out of proportion to a man's body. He lifted the tower of flesh until it rested against Erasmus's chin, swelling thicker and thicker. Paxton's one hand could only rub the flesh now. It was like rubbing one of Rocky's biceps. Despite its incredible size, the sailor's penis was sensitive. It was only a minute longer before Paxton felt the recoil of orgasm. Pointing straight in the air, it became a sprinkler, raining down heavy droplets of white rain.

Erasmus made no sound. Paxton realized the sailor had fainted.

As quickly as the massive log of flesh had swollen, it began to deflate. Erasmus regained consciousness and pushed away from Paxton. He began the long, complicated task of replacing his penis in his pants. An uncomfortable silence between the two men was broken by a customer who glanced at the two men, shrugged, and stepped to the trough to pee. Both sailors stared at the customer's plump, slightly larger than average penis, and felt a deep, hopeless envy.

BUNKMATES LOOK OUT FOR ONE ANOTHER

❦ 24 ❦

BUNKMATES LOOK OUT FOR
ONE ANOTHER

It was late when the two sailors stumbled up the gangway. Their giggling stopped suddenly when the captain appeared out of nowhere and smacked Paxton hard.

"Where the fuck have you been, boy? I told you to stay out of trouble! I sent the port police out looking for you!"

Erasmus put himself between Paxton and the captain. "Hey! He was out with me. What gives you the right?"

The captain shoved Erasmus and gave a snarl. "You know I have every right. He isn't safe out there."

"Oh, and he's safe when he's imprisoned in your cuddy? Really, captain, you've sunk to a new low. Now please step aside, sir, so my roommate and I can get some rest."

Erasmus held Paxton by the arm and pushed past the captain. He stopped short when the captain yanked the boy away from him.

"You want to spend some time in the brig, sailor? I can arrange it."

Erasmus stood his ground. "You'll send for the port police? I'll go get them, and we can sort this out."

With a shove, the captain released Paxton to Erasmus. "The police won't be here when we leave port, sailor."

Paxton resented being a pawn in this battle. He cleared his throat. "Captain, I'm well enough to sleep in my own bunk now, thank you."

The captain growled, "You know it isn't about your health. It's about my needs. I need you, boy."

"Well, you know where to find me. It's a ship. I'm not going anywhere while we're at sea."

The captain pointed at Erasmus. "This is your doing. You better sleep with one eye open."

Back in the room, Paxton wrung his hands. "I'm sorry, Erasmus. This is my fault."

"The blame lies squarely with the bastard who kept you imprisoned against your will. That is despicable."

"He just didn't let me have sex with anyone but him. It was for my protection."

Erasmus punched the ladder. "Damn it, Pax! He said it himself. It was for his gratification. You were his sex slave. Don't apologize for him."

Paxton couldn't stop stealing glances at the long bulge in his roommate's trousers. It was the longest, thickest cock he had ever seen. It held so much power and sexual energy.

"I'll be your sex slave. I want you to fill me with your cock, more than I've ever been filled before."

Paxton saw the bulge jump. He knew Erasmus liked that idea.

"You're crazy." Erasmus said it with conviction, but to Paxton, it sounded hollow.

Paxton bent over to pick up a sock from the floor. He stayed bent over a second longer than necessary. He tossed the sock in the hamper. When he turned back to Erasmus, the bulge was swelling. He stepped forward and put one hand on the sailor's big cock. He closed his eyes and waited for lips to meet his. They did. Erasmus held the ordinary seaman's head and pushed his tongue into his mouth. They stayed locked in an embrace, kissing passionately, for several minutes. Paxton's under-clothes dampened with pre-come. A wet spot developed just below the knee and spread across Erasmus's pant leg. The seams of his trousers strained as stitches popped. They both wanted to say something to the other, but they were too focused on the kiss to interrupt that perfect moment. Each man held doubts if they could follow through with what came next. Paxton was determined to relax and stretch enough to give Erasmus all the pleasure his commanding cock deserved, but he doubted he could. Erasmus was afraid he would rip Paxton open, killing him. But nothing was said.

With a loud rip, the inseam of Erasmus's trousers burst open, releasing his cock upwards. It hit Paxton right between the legs. Paxton gasped when the massive log of flesh battered his tiny balls, and he doubled over.

Paxton groaned, but Erasmus guffawed.

"I'm sorry, Pax. I can't control it,"

Paxton joined him in laughter until they both were overcome with it. They wiped tears from the corners of their eyes and laughed some more. Trip next door pounded the wall. They had to stop. Erasmus solved it by leaning in and kissing Paxton with his tongue. Whatever love Paxton had for Brick, it was ten times as powerful with Erasmus. He put his hand on his roommates colossal dick, watching it swell and lengthen with each beat of his heart.

Paxton would rather die fucking Erasmus than go on living enduring the captain. Despite Erasmus's protests, the young recruit removed his dungarees and positioned the handsome sailor's grapefruit-sized head at his hole.

Erasmus said, "You're gonna need lubrication."

Paxton shook his head. The Vaseline from earlier

that day was still coating his insides. He took a deep breath and pushed back. No movement.

Erasmus grabbed a tube of Brylcreem from his dresser drawer and applied it liberally to the head and the shaft before wiping the rest inside Paxton's loose anus.

Paxton pushed back with all his might, but the monstrous cock would not push past his opening.

Erasmus shook his head. "Forget it, kid. I'll always be a virgin. Ain't fucked man or woman my whole life."

Paxton popped a tube of amyl nitrate. As the fumes did their work, his inner sphincter relaxed. With a violent shove, Paxton tugged and forced the Able Seaman's wide cock into his well-worn rectum.

Erasmus gasped. Paxton inhaled a second whiff and forced the massive head to the back of his rectum. The Erasmus still had many inches to go. Paxton couldn't get the captain to pop past the sigmoid valve, so he worried Erasmus would never know the pleasures of his colon. That wasn't right. The captain didn't deserve to go all the way, but Paxton longed to take the blue-eyed sailor's giant all the way.

Erasmus was astounded. Until a moment ago, he was a virgin top man. Now his cock was surrounded by warm, slippery flesh. He heaved and lunged, enjoying sex for the first time in his twenty-five years on Earth. It was all too much; without warning, he spewed his come inside the younger man.

He began to deflate. That gave Paxton the chance he needed. He pushed against the semi-hard log of flesh until it popped into his colon.

"Holy crap! Did I just tear you open?"

Paxton slammed his rump into the man's pelvis, forcing him deep inside, then leaned back and kissed Erasmus. In moments, the older sailor was hard again. The soft walls of Paxton's ass stretched to accommodate the immense girth at the base of the cock. In his colon, the head swelled so large, it felt like gas pains. They were locked together in a rhythmic embrace. Erasmus pulled his cock out until the corona reached the junction; he was trapped and couldn't pull out until he got off again. He could still slide in and out five inches or so. Paxton loved the sensation when the head snagged at the exit to his sigmoid colon.

Erasmus pushed and pulled his broad flesh filling him completely then retreating hundreds of times.

"Paxton, you're a miracle."

The younger sailor rotated and lay back on the bunk, giving Erasmus full access to fuck him hard. He encouraged his impaler by spanking his muscular butt and tweaking his meaty nipples.

The come from earlier began leaking out of the hole, lubricating the immense cock and sending Erasmus into a frenzy. He pumped his meat in and out in long thrusts. Paxton put his ankles on Erasmus's shoulders. Erasmus lifted them high to gain more traction. He let an ankle drop and twisted Paxton to one side. In the new position, Paxton's guts compressed, gripping the massive cock even more tightly. Paxton was pinching his partner's nipples when the twist happened. He saw stars from glorious pain. He pinched very hard until Erasmus let out a holler. Upon release, the nipples sent a shockwave throughout Erasmus's nervous system, triggering another orgasm.

"Oh Paxton, oh sweet Jesus I'm gonna come."

Paxton pulled the older sailor to meet his lips. They searched each other's mouths with their tongues. Paxton exploded, splattering Erasmus's chest and belly. A second later, Erasmus unleashed a second flood.

"Ohhh! Fuck you're good!"

Paxton blushed at the compliment as his sigmoid colon filled with warm semen,

They stayed locked together, panting and kissing

intermittently. The kisses triggered Erasmus to swell again.

Paxton grasped the man's buttocks firmly and shoved him all the way in. Erasmus has never fucked anyone, and now he was on his third go with Paxton.

After thirty minutes of constant humping, Erasmus came a third time. Paxton wanted to kiss Erasmus so badly, but they both knew it would swell him up again and they would be locked. Instead, they waited until Erasmus deflated, allowing Paxton to expel the invading tube of flesh from his body. It snaked and coiled its way out of him, followed by a raging river of come,

They put on towels and went down the hall to the showers to remove the sweat, Vaseline, semen and Brylcreem from their tingling bodies.

❧ 25 ❧

CAPE HORNY

The roommates made love at every opportunity. The decision had to be quick; if they hesitated, Erasmus would grow too hard and his head wouldn't fit through the inner door. They spent all free time locked in the room, fucking until their skin burned from the friction. They lost count somewhere between Rio and Montevideo.

In Uruguay, the men hoped the tramp steamer would get an order for the Caribbean, but it was a large order to be delivered around the Horn in Valparaiso. The crew was disheartened. Any trip to the Pacific meant hassles. Getting from the Pacific back to the Atlantic Seaboard was never a straight path. Worst of all, their itinerary sent them through the dreaded Straits of Magellan. In modern times, it was much safer, but it still claimed several ships a year. The Panama Canal was far enough from Uruguay that the tramp steamer would lose money if they didn't make the perilous passage.

At Cape Horn, a gale became a nasty storm. Paxton had never been through such an ordeal, having only known calm seas thus far. He stayed in the room clinging to Erasmus for comfort until his stomach could bear no more. He rode the railing, nearly washing overboard as he emptied his stomach. A pair of strong, familiar arms encircled him and dragged him to the cuddy. The captain was soaking wet and furious.

"Paxton! Do you know how close you came to dying just now!?"

Paxton had dry heaves; he couldn't focus on the words.

The captain gave him some Dramamine which he quickly vomited. Only after he swallowed a few Morphine pills was he able to keep down liquids. Paxton knew that the moment he was well, he would be required to service the thickening log in the captain's pants.

The captain bent him over a chair and stripped him of his pants in a single yank. He hauled out his swollen cock and coated it with Vaseline. Paxton was relieved when the captain entered him without pain. He'd been at it with Erasmus so constantly, he had gained the ability to take a huge cock without flinching.

"Your roommate's prepared you well, son."

Paxton stifled a sigh. In and out, in and out, banging hard against his bladder, the captain's cock slid inside Paxton like a hot knife through butter. Without any thought, Paxton raised a leg and let the captain push into his colon.

"Christ! Did I just rip you open?"

Paxton shook his head. Now that he was in all the way, the captain could give Paxton real pleasure. The old man went wild, exploring the new territory like a child at an amusement park. Paxton put on his best whore act. "Oh sir, you're so powerful. You're making me come."

"You like that?"

"Uh-huh."

Paxton tugged on the meaty nipples to force an early release.

"Oh yeah. Here it comes!"

The first glob of sperm shot into Paxton just as a

fierce knock came at the door. The captain ignored it; nobody disturbed him in the cuddy. Another hot load of come spurted up inside Paxton when the door opened. It was Rocky.

"Sir! You're needed at the helm!"

"What is the meaning of this!" But Rocky didn't get to answer; there was a terrible crash and the ship threw all three men violently to the floor.

RAMMED DEEP

The next sixteen hours were a blur for Paxton. He remembered pulling his pants up. Rocky dragged him into a lifeboat with Erasmus and George. In the storm, nothing was visible except a distant light, the Faro de Punta Delgada. Erasmus, George, Rocky and Paxton paddled desperately through the troubled waters until at last they saw a spit of land covered with Penguins. The ship-to-shore radio had alerted the Coast Guard. They were on hand to pull the four men to shore. First, they handed everyone a blanket and a warm brew inside a gourd. They called it "Ma-tay". It warmed his insides and gave him renewed strength. Swaddled in blankets, the shivering sailors boarded a school bus to drive them two hours to the Hospital in Punta Arenas.

According to accounts in the papers, The Southern Cross had struck a rock in the straits between Punta Delgada and Punta Espora. Everyone survived. The captain, however, was unable to explain what had happened, so there were investigations. While Paxton rested in his hospital bed, a doctor came to examine his "culo". During the investigation, Rocky told the truth, that he found the captain fucking the young sailor when he should have been steering the ship. The doctor's report confirmed repeated assault with a very large object. The captain's cock, clearly outlined in his white pants, was the smoking gun that sealed his fate. Paxton was never asked to corroborate the story. It was considered rape by maritime law, and Paxton was a victim, not a criminal. Paxton defended the captain against the rape charges, but he couldn't deny that their final act of copulation was directly responsible for putting the Southern Cross at the bottom of the Magellan Straits. When Paxton tried to own some of the blame, the captain stopped him.

"You're OS, son. I'm the ship's captain. The fault lies with me.

Punta Arenas was quaint. It was the biggest city below the 50th Parallel, yet only about the size of Biloxi. The beaches were dotted with penguins that slipped in and out of the chilly water like it was a hot bath.

Erasmus and Paxton were assigned to the next ship to come into the Magallanes Shipyard. The Black Cat 13, bound for Valaparaiso, Costa Rica, Acapulco and San Francisco, was a dirty, run-down vessel, but the crew were welcoming of the stranded sailors. George and Rocky bid the two farewell. They were waiting for a ship headed East, back up the coast and into US Waters. Paxton shed some tears remembering the kindness these two had shown him. They were like older brothers. Rocky said, "We're brothers of the sea. We'll see each other again on one ship or another."

In a surprising turn of events, the sailors were given the First Mate's room, which had a large double bed.

"Sorry, fellas, we don't have any bunk beds left. You'll have to make do."

And make do they did. Once secured in their room on the Black Cat, the two men gave off electric sparks. Although the waters had given them a chill, they were quickly heating up. Erasmus locked the door.

Silently, they stripped their clothes. Erasmus let his hardening cock out of its prison. Paxton lay back on the big bed, his legs jutting skyward. He grabbed a bottle of lubricating jelly he lifted from his hospital room. He inserted the nozzle into his anus and squeezed a generous helping. Erasmus spit in his hand several times and slicked up his dong.

"You sure you want this?"

"I can't get enough."

Gently at first, then with increasing force, Erasmus dug his way into the warm hole. He made an audible "pop" when the corona snapped past the inner sphincter.

"Oh jeez. Oh man." Paxton shuddered with ecstasy. It was one thing to have the attention of the sexiest sailor on the seven seas, and quite another to stuff his rectum with the biggest cock on the water.

Paxton's eyes grew foggy and a tear trickled down his cheek.

"Hey, Pax, are you okay?"

"I dreamed about you from the moment I first saw you in N'Awlins. I didn't think dreams came true for the son of a hooker."

"I dreamt about this beauty," Erasmus pointed to Paxton's butt. "And now I'm claiming it. The sea brought us together."

"Speaking of together," Paxton said, then pulled Erasmus hard to force him into his colon.

Erasmus forgot how good it felt to go all the way. Now his mid-shaft was being massaged by the bend between the rectum and Paxton's guts. His blue eyes sparkled with delight.

Paxton, overcome with pleasure, rolled his eyes back in his head and lay back on the pillow. Erasmus followed him there, planting his lips on his and kissing him the French way.

Erasmus pushed him onto his side and took him

from behind. This gave him the deepest access, filling Paxton with his gargantuan cock.

Like a woman, Paxton began to quake with anal orgasm. His entrails massaged Erasmus in rhythmic waves. Paxton moaned aloud in ecstasy.

Erasmus didn't need to do anything. The sensation was so powerful, it caused him to come without any effort. Hot semen coated Paxton's lower digestive tract. It warmed his entrails. The rhythmic spasms of his colon gave way to ejaculation. His come fired out of his tiny penis in an arc and cleared the bed, landing on the desk across the room.

Erasmus, shrinking in the wake of his orgasm, saw Paxton's high-flying come; immediately he stiffened again, lodging himself deep inside once more.

"Paxton, holy crap. You must have broken a record! You got me all turned on again. I'm stuck."

Paxton rotated to a missionary position, wrapping his long legs around the sailor's wide body. "I guess there's only one thing left to do."

And they did it. Day and night, and during the lunch hour when possible, the two men found erotic bliss in bed, in the bathroom, in the kitchen, anywhere they could manage a quick fuck or a long, slow lovemaking session. Paxton's lips were chapped and red from Erasmus's powerful kisses. As happens in a deepening relationship, they found the initial penetration increasingly swift. No pain, just a little spit and Erasmus slipped into Paxton's deepest recesses. By the time the ship pulled into San Francisco, they were in love.

THE END

EPILOGUE

Erasmus and Paxton, or Razz and Pax as they were known in the neighborhood, rented a cottage in the Latin Quarter at the foot of Telegraph Hill in San Francisco. In that part of town, there were a lot of busy bars and cafes that catered to sailors and others of their kind. They were very popular at the Black Cat, where male beauty in all its forms was applauded and appreciated. The two never went on a voyage without the other. They were close to the piers and could always enlist on a vessel bound for an exotic destination. Japan, Thailand and Singapore were long voyages, giving the two sailors plenty of time alone together on the open sea.

Like all marriages, there came a time when they needed variety. Erasmus was secure in his masculinity; he often allowed a third to enter the marriage and spend time inside them both. Nobody ever dared to do more than touch the giant that lurked in Razz's sailor pants. It was a formula for marital bliss known mainly to gay men. The outsider brought new blood into the marriage and reinvigorated the love between them.

They're together still, in North Beach - living legends. To supplement their income, they give shows in the salons of the curious who demand proof that

Paxton is the most skilled passive homosexual in the City. To this day, he is the only one who can take Erasmus at all, let alone completely. Some of the well-to-do on Nob Hill pay as much as a thousand dollars a show. A few photographs and super-8 films have been recorded and circulated. You may see them someday in a magazine, at a peep show, or tucked between the sticky pages of a novel not unlike this one.

❧ III ❧
PANAMA HEAT
BY PETER SCHUTES

ABOUT PANAMA HEAT

BY PETER SCHUTES

<u>Panama Heat</u> is a fictional tale set in the very real Culebra Cut, an engineering project along the Panama Canal. It required carving a river through the Continental Divide. The men who went were divided by Gold and Silver, the two-class system based on race and ethnicity. Peter remembered this inequality from his childhood when his father brought his family to the Culebra Cut to live in one of the Gold Villages where married white Americans could keep their family together. The Gold Bachelor colonies and all Silver housing were male-only environments. Having seen these bachelor quarters firsthand as a young boy, he filed them away in his imagination for later fictionalization in this book.

Peter spoke often of the "inner chamber" or the "second room." Even in this early work, the narrative focuses intensely on this second sphincter between the rectum and the sigmoid colon. Apocryphal accounts of Peter's sexual escapades confirmed that his enormous endowment was a frequent visitor to men's "inner rooms." He is reputed to have once said, "If you can't get there, you should take a passive role and let the big boys take you there instead."

❋   I   ❋

VIEUX CARRÉ

Quentin Fournier of the New Orleans Fourniers was an adventurer at heart. Nearly all of his family were very much the opposite - conservative, stay-at-home Confederates still mourning the loss of the Civil War. Quentin wanted nothing more than to escape the oppressive household and find his fortune in distant lands. His mother and father did not understand him; his brothers and sisters despised him. Only his Aunt Lisette, an eccentric who never married, understood Quentin's unusual passions.

She told him, "People rarely tolerate different things, for the unusual makes them fear they will stray from the herd. Don't let people define who you should be. Listen only to your heart."

Quentin took this admonition as gospel. One night in early 1904, his heart was whispering the name of a bar in the Vieux Carré. The Curzon was a popular hangout for sailors and enterprising women. Not every sailor had the money nor the inclination to pay for these women's services. Quentin had no need of money, and his handsome face drew interest from the randy sailors searching for a good time. The Curzon had a rooming house right upstairs. It always had vacancies because they offered discounts on rooms rented by the hour.

Quentin entered the smoky bar and chose a barstool with a view of the entrance. It was early yet. He wanted to study his quarry.

The whores tolerated Quentin; they didn't want to befriend a pervert. They kept a cool distance, but they cooperated. Quentin sent talkative men of no persuasion to the nest of prostitutes across the bar, and they returned the favor whenever they clocked a john as a molly.

A steamboat full of Midwestern merchant marines tied up on the docks near the French Market. Within minutes a steady stream of seamen poured into the bar in search of carnal pleasures. Many handsome rakes passed Quentin by in search of a warm bosom. Quentin knew to expect some disappointment in the presence of the harlots. A sailor entered. The bar breathed a collective gasp for two reasons: the man was handsome, and he was big as a house. With each step, his thigh muscles bulged and strained against his white cotton pants. His broad shoulders were attached to arms bigger than Quentin's legs.

The sailor tipped his hat at Quentin and sat his enormous buttocks one stool over.

He extended a sinewy hand. "Jacob Ayers."

"Quentin Fournier." He gulped.

Jacob smiled. "Don't worry, friend. I may be big, but I'm gentle as a kitten."

"How did you get so big?"

"Lifting barrels of sardines for ten hours a day. Feel that." Jacob flexed his bicep, tearing at the fabric of his shirt sleeve. Quentin put both hands around the sailor's massive arm, but his fingers would not touch.

Quentin was skilled in the art of seduction. He

knew when to stop talking. He held the man's arm for several seconds, studying his face.

Jacob grinned. "Here, feel that." He moved Quentin's hands to his pectoral muscles. He flexed them one at a time in rapid succession.

Quentin whistled. "Holy Cow." Again, he left his hands on the man far longer than most would.

This was the moment. He smiled at Jacob, then let his eyes roam downward until they reached the crotch. He glanced at his prey, who never stopped smiling.

"Is it big like the rest of you"?

Jacob nodded.

❦

UPSTAIRS, QUENTIN WATCHED THE MUSCLEMAN undress. His torso was unlike any he had seen. Dozens of tiny muscles rippled in unison as he folded his shirt. He grabbed Quentin's shirt front and yanked it off, exposing Quentin's thin, wiry frame. Quentin felt pressure on his knee; it was Jacob's prick growing big and hard, straining against the pants.

Quentin unbuttoned the sailor pants on the left and right until they were loose enough to move. He tugged hard until they dislodged from the huge shelf of an ass. The legs were tight, so he had to work on them one at a time to prevent them from bunching up. The last hurdle was the cock, which leaped gracefully skyward once freed from its cloth prison.

Jacob's cock was large. It appeared smaller framed against those meaty thighs, but it was a whopper. Quentin took the man's stiff shaft in his mouth. He tongued it with abandon. It tasted like a beignet. He sucked and slurped, allowing the thick meat to work its way to the back of his throat. There he let it slip past his tonsils and enter the throat. Jacob gasped.

"How did you do that?"

Quentin had his mouth full and couldn't answer. Instead, he kept doing it until the muscled sailor grabbed him by the ears.

"Stop. I'm close. Let's fuck."

Quentin let the thick cock out of his mouth with a pop. He unbuttoned his pants, turning away from the man as he did so.

"Now hold on there, boy, I wanna see yours too."

"It's of little interest."

He whirled Quentin around, exposing his tiny penis. He guffawed.

"How do you fuck your wife with that little thing?"

"Like this," Quentin said, turning back so his ass was exposed. He pulled the cheeks apart to show off his perfect puckered hole.

Jacob spat liberally into his hand. He worked a finger into Quentin's spit-slick backside. Quentin wriggled and let out a sigh.

"This might hurt," Jacob warned. He pressed the apricot-sized head of his penis against Quentin's hole. The boy's puckered anus spread to accommodate the invasion. With some surprise, Jacob continued sliding into him with no protest. He was buried to the hilt.

Quentin had nerve endings that sent powerful messages whenever a man's cock came in contact with them. His pleasure depended on the other man. For that reason, he rotated until he was in a modified missionary, staring into his invader's dark eyes.

Jacob stared back as he started rocking his hips, sliding deep into the boy. It felt good, so he closed his eyes and moaned.

That blind moan was the trigger Quentin needed. His nerves were on fire with pleasure. He caressed Jacob's nipples. The burly man grabbed his wrist and placed the hand squarely on his nipple.

"Pinch me hard."

Quentin obliged, and more moans from the sailor sent reverberating waves of arousal echoing through him. His anus began contracting in spasms of delight. The sailor fucked harder. Quentin could see the man's perfectly round butt rising and falling with each stroke. He grabbed hold with both hands, feeling the muscles rippling beneath his fingers. He wandered to the small of the back, where the man's thrusting got its added strength.

Jacob had never fucked like this. No man or woman ever let him ravage them with complete abandon until now. Quentin had a dick-shaped asshole, perfect for fucking. He occasionally thrust hard enough to hit the end of the rectum, causing Quentin to gasp.

"Am I hurting you? I don't want to hurt you."

"Fuck me harder. As hard as you want."

Quentin's permission was all he needed. He lifted and carried him, impaled, around the shabby room. Quentin bounced and wiggled. Jacob wanted to kiss him, but it was wrong.

Quentin read his mind. He leaned forward and locked lips with the sailor. That was too much pleasure. The end was approaching.

It started with Quentin. His twitching anus stimulated his balls; he leaked clear fluid onto Jacob's rippled stomach.

Jacob felt the juice on his belly. It excited him. He made the boy leak like a woman. He sat on the bed, with Quentin riding him like a huge muscled horse. Quentin pinched and twisted both nipples, sending Jacob over the edge of the falls.

"Oh, my god, oh, god, I'm close, man."

Quentin planted his feet on the ground to allow him to slide up and down the man's cock faster.

"Oh yes! Here it comes!" Quentin felt a fiery hot

flood of muscleman sperm splatter inside him. The man's sudden release triggered his own orgasm. Quentin shot sperm up onto the shoulders and nipples of the sailor. Jacob laughed in astonishment.

"You'll have kids. It's the bullets, not the gun."

To shut him up, Quentin kissed him again.

IN THE POKEY

The night was still young. Jacob moved on to another bar; Quentin went downstairs on the prowl for another fuck. He needed to move quickly; he didn't want the sailor's sperm to leak out of him. There is no better lubricant than another man's sperm.

The bar was busy. Quentin wanted a different experience this time. Muscles like Jacob's are incredible. They're sexy. But Quentin would take a skinny weakling over muscles if the guy had a horse cock. Quentin was excited by size. Jacob was big, but he wasn't huge.

Quentin surveyed the room at crotch level. He wasn't sure he would find a colossal cock tonight. Things looked pretty normal down there.

His eyes landed on a man in linen pants. Down below, there was something abnormally large. This was a soft cock, hanging about a third of the way to his knee. Attached to the prize was a nondescript man with a dull mustache and boring blue eyes. The man approached Quentin. His luck tonight was incredible.

"Hey. I saw you looking at my..."

"I was. It's hard to miss."

The man blushed. "Why are you looking?"

Quentin wasn't sure if he should answer. Instead, he asked, "Are you looking"?

"I don't follow." God, this man was dense. He decided to be brazen.

"I just got fucked. He was strong, but he came up short. That meat of yours could satisfy me."

More blushing. "Okay, let's go upstairs."

Quentin smiled. It worked. Judging by the looks of it, he wouldn't be able to walk right after tonight.

They stepped out into the cold night air.

"Let's hurry. I still have his come inside me. You'll love how it feels."

As he was chattering away, Quentin failed to notice the man signaling to a friend down the block. Then came the cold metallic click of handcuffs. The policeman's companion joined him.

"You are under arrest for crimes against nature." The two men walked Quentin to the nearby police station, making hateful remarks. The cop removed the rolled sock from his pant leg.

Quentin laughed. "You needed a prop! I'll bet yours is even smaller than mine!" Then he felt a terrible pain in his head; the lights went out.

❧

THIS WAS NOT QUENTIN'S FIRST ARREST. HE HAD embarrassed his family many times. He would still be rotting in prison had not the Fourniers forked out a lot of money to the Policeman's Ball every year.

No one came to bail him out this time. The cops kept him alone in his cell. They taunted him, offering up their inadequate penises while hurling epithets so blue it caused other prisoners to blush. If Quentin had been dreaming of adventure, it was now redoubled with his desire to escape to a new climate less hostile to his predilections. With each passing day, his need for adventure became an obsession.

Eventually, Harold Boyer, the Chief of Police, learned of the prisoner's identity and ordered him released immediately. The rude jailers escorted Quentin to the Chief's office.

The Chief waved them away, leaving Quentin alone with the man. Chief Boyer shook his head.

"Quentin Fournier, your antics are giving New Orleans and your family a bad name. I have known you since you were born. Our families sit in the same salons and attend the same operas. Your shame is spreading. What do you have to say for yourself?"

Quentin had plenty to say, but he bit his tongue. He looked into the gray-haired man's eyes, studying them. Chief Boyer looked down below his desk. He raised his eyes to meet Quentin's.

"You have a choice. You can stay in New Orleans as a prisoner or take the next steamer out of town. What will it be?"

Quentin felt like Br'er Rabbit being offered a briar patch for punishment. The adventure he craved would be mandatory.

"The steamer."

"Good choice. Now, your freedom comes at a price." He tilted his head, inviting the young man to his side of the desk.

Quentin's eyes were saucers. The chief was not a young man, but his virility was visibly intact. A flesh log of obscene dimensions snaked down his pant leg.

"Son, you have a reputation that interests an old man with my problem. Help me out."

Quentin reached to unbuckle his trousers.

"No! Not your ass! You disgusting pervert. Your mouth!"

He forced Quentin to his knees and stood. He

dropped his trousers, giving Quentin a close view of the Chief's enormous cock.

Quentin struggled to wrap his mouth around the man's horse cock.

The chief thrust impatiently.

"Come on, son; this is what you do, ain't it?"

Quentin nodded. He preferred to host such monstrosities in his nether regions, but his mouth could accommodate bloated cocks like Chief Boyer's.

The chief's wife must be a saint. She had given birth to fourteen children, of which eleven survived. The Boyers were a massive clan. And they all started inside these huge testicles and sprang from his wife's vagina. Giving birth must have been easy for her, given the monster she had to host nightly.

The chief needed this act of fellatio. His wife had a delicate mouth, and he had never experienced the real thing. Her feeble licks and slick hands felt nothing like Quentin's gullet. This boy was a treasure. As his cock slid past the young man's tonsils, he felt a pang of regret at sending away such a talented cocksucker. He kept going, heedless of Quentin's tears, deeper than he'd ever been before. Not even the whores at Curzon could take his whole length. For the first time, he felt his pubic bone touch lips. He was all the way in.

Quentin feared he might faint if the Chief didn't pull out. He was deep as he could go and thrusting in short, rapid strokes. Quentin pulled back, feeling the boa constrictor cock leave his throat, allowing the air to come rushing in. Quentin took two deep breaths and went back down. In this way, he was able to continue for thirty minutes. He was aching to touch himself. Having his throat used like a cavernous vagina was exciting. His breath control brought him to the edge of consciousness, where every thrust inspired intense arousal. Spots appeared before his eyes. He withdrew for two more breaths, then, for the hundredth time, he impaled his head on the fleshy stake of cop meat. His vision returned to normal, briefly.

The chief closed his eyes. The soft moaning grew louder. Quentin realized he didn't need to touch himself. Providing his services to a man who needed them so severely was causing his tiny penis to leak fluid. He knew this meant his own orgasm was assured. He tasted that salty foretaste that preceded the flood. The chief buried his brutal billy club of a cock all the way, thrusting in ever shorter strokes. Quentin could not unblock his airway now. The Chief was oblivious to the plight of his oral savior. Quentin tapped then slapped the chief's thighs, but the train had left the station. Quentin could feel salty liquid oozing down his raw throat, coating it until it became a slick tunnel for the chief to violate easily.

Quentin gave up his silent pleas for air. He fondled the man's prolific testicles, stimulating a muscle that every man knew. It was the muscle that contracts to draw the ball sac upward on cold days. Quentin felt the muscle quiver and pump.

The Chief hollered, "Yes, oh fuck I'm there. Sweet Jesus, I'm there!" And Quentin felt the fluid begin its long journey from that muscle to the end of the flesh firehose. It was so arousing to swallow all of this man's would-be children that Quentin had his first hands-free orgasm from oral sex. The last thing he remembered before passing out was a warm river of sperm rushing down his throat into his empty stomach.

❧ 3 ❧

PANAMA BOUND

When Quentin awoke, he was sitting on a bench a block from the police station. His pants were stained with his own orgasm. It was time to go home and pack his bags. He had no destination in mind.

Walking along Chartres Street in the Faubourg Marigny, Quentin spied a poster announcing jobs in Panama. White Americans were given free transportation, housing, and generous pay in exchange for labor on the great canal being built. Quentin followed the directions to the warehouse where the hiring was happening; he signed up on the spot.

Upon learning of his plans, his immediate family heaved a collective sigh of relief. Aunt Lisette was terribly worried for him. She invited him to tea. It soothed his violated throat and inflamed tonsils.

"Quentin, they say men there are dying by the thousands because of yellow fever and malaria."

Quentin shrugged it off. The brochure explained how every house was fully screened against mosquitos, recently discovered to be the source of these fevers.

"I'm not afraid. The Americans are on the job now; they know how to do things right. I will be protected against mosquitoes in my home.

"But when you labor in the field, what then?"

"Labor in the field? I'm not going to do such work. Do not worry, Auntie, I will find work in the accounting offices, in line with my training at college."

Several days later, with minimal ceremony, Quentin boarded an ocean-going steamship, the Bayou Prince, bound for Panama.

The Prince was segregated. White Americans with British, Teutonic, or French backgrounds were given private rooms above deck. They were separated from Blacks, Italians, and Spaniards. It was just how things were done. But Quentin had a fondness for all men, be they White, Black, Spanish, or Italian, and he would frequently find excuses to go below board and mingle with the swarthier men. They had better liquor, played better cards, and made for better friends than his snobby white counterparts above deck. Here, he learned about "Silver and Gold," the caste system that ensured separation between White Americans and everyone else. While Quentin would be paid in American Gold coins, the others were paid in Panamanian Silver coins. It was necessary because Spaniards and Italians could pass for white, so they should have only silver to spend to ensure they remained in their proper caste.

The journey to Panama would take 15 days. In the first few days, the visits with the men were convivial and friendly, as Quentin expected. About five days into the journey, the absence of women on board was causing a change in the men. This was what Quentin had dreamed of when he signed up. There was a predatory gleam in the eyes of many passengers below deck. His stuffy White counterparts were far too puritanical to admit to their ever-growing needs, but the men downstairs were brazen. Quentin laughed along to their many crude jokes. Soon, he would let these men know he was available to them to serve their deepest, most private desires. He dropped subtle hints to seed the field. With ten more days until touching land, the smorgasbord of repressed male sensuality would be a king's feast.

However, on the sixth day, when Quentin planned to drop the charade and start his conquest, the voyage took an unexpected turn that could have drastically set back his plans. The steamer touched ground at Progreso to gather fuel. The men were allowed out for six hours. The brothels were at capacity, absorbing male lust like a sea sponge. But they gave priority to White men with gold coins. Only a few of the silver payroll could find release in the wake of the white tide. Sixty-five satisfied men returned to the ship, leaving another two hundred aching for release. It turned out that the detour only increased Quentin's odds of success.

❧ 4 ❧

MASSIMO'S SALAMI

As the ship raised anchor, Quentin stole away to the Italian quarters. The air was filled with the fragrance of frustration. Quentin marched up to Massimo, a short, muscular Roman with a visible blessing below his belt. Massimo's eyes narrowed. Men rarely accosted one another unless they were picking a fight. Quentin brushed his legs against Massimo's. He whispered a few words and walked away, into the galley.

It was late; the kitchen was inoperative. Quentin found the pantry. He located a container of lard. He lowered his linen pants and bent over a stack of flour sacks, his pink rump exposed and waiting. He liberally applied lard to his asshole. Not two minutes later, Massimo lumbered in. He lowered his dungarees, revealing a colossal cock. It was nearly as big around as it was long. It rivaled the dry salami swinging from the rafters. Quentin suppressed a scream as Massimo penetrated him. Despite his skill and experience, there were some men he could not accommodate without crippling pain. They were much thicker than ordinary men and required patience. Few ever had it. They would plunge their cocks into him with little regard for his comfort. But in every case, the searing pain vanished as intense satisfaction took its place.

Massimo's cock did not grow comfortable inside him right away. Quentin's brow was covered in a cold sweat. His shallow breaths betrayed the agony he endured. Massimo was inexperienced and brutal. He had no technique. But men were Quentin's weakness. He grew drunk from their lascivious attention. Massimo's selfish conquest became a cordial for Quentin's pain. With the pounding warmth of his giant cock, lard melted and ran down their legs, forming a puddle at their feet.

As Massimo's thrusts grew longer, Quentin reveled in the sublime sliding sensation stretching and stimulating his hole. He wondered if women felt this same tingling satisfaction or if they just spread their legs, ignored the ensuing violation, and thought about something else. Massimo's merciless cock would be impossible to ignore. Immense, cruel and deep, it would leave any hole loose and flapping in the wind.

Massimo was furry. Quentin loved the wooly chest hair scratching his smooth back. The giant bush of pubic hair rubbed across his smooth buttocks. Massimo grunted and slapped Quentin's beautiful backside. Quentin tightened his anus in response, squeezing the massive member ravaging his insides.

Massimo was all brute strength and had no technique. For Quentin, every man was a new delight. Whether they were highly skilled or clumsy oafs, small, medium, or large, each one became a token to add to his treasure chest of conquests. Some were more enjoyable than others. What Massimo lacked in skill, he made up for in size and force.

No matter how clumsy, every man finds his rhythm sometime before he approaches climax. Massimo was no exception. He grabbed hold of Quentin's hips and thrust in ever-intensifying strokes. Quentin felt himself completely stuffed, then quickly emptied, over and over in rapid succession. Massimo's thick tool bumped hard into the bottom of his rectum. It was painful and delicious at the same time. Quentin leaked clear fluid from his soft penis. He always did. He remained soft to allow his partner's cock to take center stage. Quentin was not big, well below average, but a hard cock of any size can disgust a man when he's fucking and thinking about women. This was all part of Quentin's skill. He had a unique talent for bringing new pleasures to men who preferred women.

Massimo was the beneficiary of these skills. Silent until now, he finally spoke, "You better than the woman."

Quentin agreed with a groan of lust.

Massimo fucked Quentin harder and harder. "Woman no can take me. They cry. Not you."

"I know what a man wants, not just what he needs."

Massimo pushed Quentin against the flour sacks to brace him for the onslaught. He pounded him with the ferocity of hand-to-hand combat. It felt as though Massimo were punching him inside. Massimo's thick fingers tightened on his flesh and raised welts. Quentin wanted to cry out in pain, but the fucking felt too good. Being joined at the waist, another man's flesh invading his, was the ultimate pleasure. Quentin gently thrust backward to meet Massimo's violent blows. This, he knew, would please the brute, for women would no doubt pull away from him at this critical moment when he was lost in fucking, ready to topple into orgasm.

Quentin's instincts were correct, informed by hundreds of encounters like this. Massimo pushed deeply into him, making him leak ropes of clear fluid that stained the flour sacks. The Italian gave a final thrust, groaned, and then released a six-day load of come into Quentin. He collapsed across Quentin's back, dripping sweat from his thatch of body hair.

Some men would want to see Quentin orgasm. It would convince them they had done a good job. Massimo was greedy and didn't care. Quentin preferred the selfish men who fucked him only for their own needs.

Still hard, Massimo pulled his massive cock out of Quentin's rear end and let it smack hard on his back. It felt like a heavy beef tenderloin being dropped on him.

Massimo neither cuddled nor kissed. He wiped the dripping end of his cock on Quentin's backside, pulled up his dungarees, and turned to leave.

On the threshold, he asked, "You want I send my friends"?

Quentin grinned over his shoulder. "Yes, Please."

EDUARDO'S ANATOMY
LESSON

Quentin stayed prone on the flour sacks all night while the crew of Italian beasts violated his mouth, hands, and anus. He lost count of how many men whitewashed his insides with their spew. Near dawn, the men left Quentin lying in a heap, drenched in their fluids. He pulled on his linen trousers and stumbled past the breakfast cooks just arriving for their shift. He slept until the afternoon.

His fame spread quickly among the lower classes below deck. His services were in such high demand that some men offered him cash. He did not need their money. He only wanted their semen deep inside him, whether in his throat or rectum. He made the pantry his office, and the flour sacks were his desk. He was open wide every night.

Massimo had been one exceptional male specimen with his powerful thick cock. But a Spaniard named Eduardo put him to shame.

From outward appearances, Eduardo, or Ed, as the others called him, was a tall, thin, homely man with deep-set eyes in a prematurely balding head. At the end of a busy evening, he appeared in Quentin's offices to find him ass out, face down in the sacks. Unlike most men, Eduardo wanted to see Quentin's face. In halting English, he asked him to turn around and lie on his back.

"Like this"? Quentin raised his legs in a V

"Sí." Eduardo grasped one ankle, lowering his pants before grabbing hold of the other.

When the Spaniard's pants dropped, Quentin gasped. Between his skinny legs was a soft fleshy battering ram, growing harder and larger with each throb. It had a standard-sized head, dwarfed by the giant hump behind it, which narrowed at the crotch. Ed was much longer than Massimo. His cock was thinner at the head and the base but much thicker in the middle.

Quentin already had lard and the sperm of a dozen men inside him, so he pulled Ed forward and inside him. Ed's cock came to a halt an inch in, for it was there that it grew far too wide for easy insertion. Ed looked into Quentin's eyes hungrily. He yearned for a connection. Despite the man's ugly appearance, Quentin enjoyed his attention. Ed put his hand on Quentin's soft cock, and began massaging it while he forced another inch into him. Quentin couldn't hide his agony. Ed pulled away. Quentin was relieved but also afraid he would scare Ed off. He scooted on the flour sacks, impaling himself again on Ed's oblong tool.

"Don't worry. Just do it."

He reached for Ed's buttocks to pull him closer, but his arms weren't long enough. Ed had many more inches to go. Ed leaned into him, slipping one, two, three inches further. Quentin pounded the flour sacks with his fists.

"Yes. Si. Keep going, Ed." It was the opposite of what his body begged. Every nerve screamed for relief. But Quentin knew relief could be closer if Ed kept pushing. Besides. What his body wanted was secondary to what the owner of the cock inside him needed. His ass was a receptacle for their pleasure. He only felt right when he was servicing another man.

Quentin's fingers finally connected with Ed, and he pulled the man closer. With an audible 'pop,' Ed's cock slipped past the tightest spot and rapidly filled Quentin. The unique shape of Ed's phallus caused it to be pressed very tightly against the bottom of Quentin's anal cavity, with seemingly nowhere to go. But Ed had technique. He knew the inside of a man's ass, its many contours, and secrets.

Quentin had endured brutal poundings from longer cocks, but he had never discovered what Ed showed him.

Ed shifted Quentin's torso at an angle and pressed forward. Quentin gasped as the massive meat shifted and turned a corner. His eyes fluttered. He groaned. What was this new sensation? It was suddenly so comfortable. Ed's cock head was holding open a gateway Quentin never knew existed. Ed's balls smacked into Quentin's behind with a final thrust, and he was entirely inside. The inner gateway was stretched wide by the club-like thickness. Quentin stared into Ed's eyes, gasping and grunting with pleasure.

Ed continued to fondle Quentin's cock, which had grown rock-hard. It oozed seminal fluid. Ed leaned forward and licked it clean. Quentin shuddered.

Ed retreated, removing perhaps five inches. It hurt terribly, but Quentin was able to hide it. Like a locomotive, Ed repeated his in and out thrusts with ever-increasing speed. Quentin thrashed and pounded, but his face was one giant smile. Ed continued to violate the usual opening, but with his deepest thrusts, the stretching moved to the interior doorway, causing ripples of pain and pleasure to travel up and down Quentin's insides.

Ed's hand stroked Quentin's little penis. Quentin couldn't initially figure out why Ed would want to do this. Men are selfish with sex. He studied Ed's eyes and understood. Ed wanted to know what it would be like to be average or even below normal in size. Quentin's little dick was a gateway to a fantasy. Knowing this allowed Quentin to relax and enjoy the hand job. His mind would not allow him to experience the joys of sex unless he gave pleasure to another. Ed's long fingers enclosing Quentin's manhood felt good for both of them.

Ed plunged in and out of Quentin. Occasionally he would miss the inner door and ram Quentin's rectum, sending familiar waves of pain along his abdomen. It all felt good.

Ed's breaths changed; he was close. Quentin felt the difference, and then a tingling built in his cock. Ed was massaging it with expert precision. Quentin rarely had a genuine orgasm, but Ed clearly needed to see it. Ed bent and took Quentin into his mouth, sucking and licking him closer to orgasm. His mouth full, Ed grunted savagely and thrust his cock completely inside Quentin, past the door, stretching it to its maximum. Moments later, a familiar warm flood filled his bowels. The thrill of being stretched so deep inside put Quentin over the edge. His little penis produced shot after shot of come. Ed held it in his mouth, then spit it in Quentin's face.

Ed's tenderness became suddenly violent as he became disgusted with himself. He smacked Quentin hard across the face and violently withdrew his still throbbing cock, only to viciously plunge it back inside him.

Quentin saw this as an opportunity to provide Ed with more pleasure, so he allowed him to punch him, fuck him, and spit on him until suddenly Ed burst into tears. He kissed Quentin forcefully. His cock remained rock hard inside. After the kiss, Ed wiped tears from his eyes. "Sorry."

Quentin rubbed his belly and stroked his buttocks. Ed grew soft. Quentin expelled the massive man from his still-tingling insides. The obscenely long, thick cock slapped Ed's thigh with an audible smack. Ed looked longingly at Quentin's little soft penis. He left abruptly, brushing past the next man in line.

❧ 6 ❧

CARLO SEEKS THE CURE

After Ed, average lengths left him disappointed. He knew his pleasure was unimportant, but he also felt he had a right to feel that inner doorway being violated for another man's pleasure. Massimo was too hard and thick to turn the corner, so he just kept pounding the painful drum of his rectum.

Besides Ed, Quentin knew only two other men who could reach that point. Black Sam, the cook, was sixty years old. He didn't like white boys but made an exception for Quentin only after the lad promised to show him something new. Quentin took him easily, for his cock was not thick, and then an astonished Sam turned the corner. Black Sam exploded almost immediately. He thanked Quentin for the anatomy lesson, then took his newfound skill and used it on the willing black men in his shared quarters.

A bald Sicilian named Carlo had a horse dick between his legs. He could never get fully erect because it would cause him to pass out. Even semi-erect, Carlo could reach and fill that hole deep within. But Quentin wasn't satisfied because Carlo had trouble enjoying sex with the fear of fainting on his mind.

Quentin solved the dilemma. In the pantry, Carlo had to be on his feet for sex. Carlo needed a safe place to lie down and let someone else do the work. They discussed it, and he agreed to a ruse. The hung Sicilian was a carpenter. He put on his tool belt and followed Quentin to his private cabin. As expected, a nosy ensign stopped them.

"What is this man doing above deck?"

"Sir, this is Carlo. He's going to repair my chest of drawers."

The ensign glared at each in turn. "All right, but be quick about it."

Inside Quentin's room, with the door locked, Carlo dropped his tool belt and trousers. Quentin pushed Carlo into the hammock.

Naked, he straddled Carlo and rubbed his rosy red butt up and down his elephantine penis. Carlo took several minutes to engorge. He was as thick as Massimo but much longer. As he got close to fully erect, his eyes fluttered.

Quentin jammed Carlo's head inside. He rubbed his silken chest hairs and the top of his bald head. Carlo smiled and grew harder. Then he fainted. But his cock remained hard. Quentin sat down hard, pushing Carlo deep inside him. Carlo woke and looked around the room. Quentin put a finger to Carlo's lips and squatted, taking another three inches of Sicilian meat inside him. With a twist and a final thrust, he took Carlo into his inner chamber. He rode the man like a pony. Carlo grew increasingly happier as he felt himself stiffen fully inside the boy.

Quentin had never seen him fully erect. His assessment that he was the same thickness as Massimo was wrong. He was much thicker. As Carlo grew inside him, he felt every interior surface stretched like a sausage casing. The inner door could scarcely accept such mass and density. Carlo wore the smile of a man experiencing his first true erection. This was what Quentin was after.

He rode Carlo like a bronco. To his embarrassment,

the experience of being inflated from the inside had caused Quentin to harden. His cock dribbled clear semen on Carlo's furry belly.

Carlo began to buck and thrust from below. Quentin expected blood; the ride was so rough. But his innards had grown calluses during these days at sea, and he held up.

Tears formed in the corners of Carlo's eyes.

"What is it, baby?"

"Am so happy." Carlo lifted Quentin to allow him room to fuck in and out of his hole at jackrabbit speed. Quentin felt climax growing in his hard untouched cock. He was ashamed until he felt Carlo put it in his mouth.

Carlo licked and sucked Quentin past the turning point. He greedily swallowed Quentin's climax.

The jackrabbit fucking slowed suddenly. Carlo moaned.

Deep inside Quentin's inner room, Carlo released a flood of baby-making sperm. Then another. And another. Carlo felt like he had come for the first time. He had never been erect during orgasm.

The volumes of semen cascaded through Quentin's stretched passageways, forced out by the pressure of Carlo's monstrous hard flesh.

Semen sprayed from Quentin with each thrust of Carlo's pump handle. The Sicilian spew traced its way through forests of thick hair. It dribbled through the hammock net to form puddles on the floor. Carlo was completely conscious. Still deep inside Quentin, he swung his legs over and stood, bear-hugging Quentin to his sweaty chest.

"Mi hai guarito! É un miracolo!" Carlo planted his lips on Quentin's. It was a kiss of joy, gratitude, and friendship. It meant more to Quentin than any other kind of kiss.

CULEBRA CUT

By the time the Bayou Prince weighed anchor at Colón, Quentin reckoned he'd taken well over a gallon of semen in his rear end. His hole was raw and tender. He was relieved to see the men abandon him for the brothels lining the shore of this boomtown. He needed time to heal. He jokingly wondered how many men would now pay the women extra to use their other hole.

After paperwork and ink stamps, Quentin caught the rail to the focus of the canal project, the Culebra Cut. It was a monumental project, abandoned by the French many years prior. It required carving a v-shaped passage through the Continental Divide. The Biblical labors needed to move mountains had taken their toll. Tens of thousands of Frenchmen had lost their lives due to poor engineering and tropical disease.

In the year since the Americans bought the rights to continue the long-abandoned project, they had taken drastic measures to improve working conditions. Married white men were permitted to move their families into villages. This kept morale high on the gold payroll. Quentin had no family, so he was relegated to another township across the canal reserved for Gold bachelors.

Fever was still common, but less so since the discovery that mosquitoes carried it. The company blanketed the countryside with DDT, reducing the mosquito population drastically. Improvements of the modern age, like sanitation, steel scaffolding, and steam-powered digging machines, further reduced the hazards at Culebra Cut.

Quentin turned heads as he walked the Main Street through the center of the bachelor village. His walk and his beautiful face made every man take notice. There were no ethnic men of color here, but Quentin didn't mind. Any man with an aching desire could become his next partner in pleasure. He was overjoyed to make his home in a village of single men, miles from the nearest brothel. He discovered that the Silver camps of Spaniards, Italians, and Negroes were less than a mile from his cabin. Women and families were not permitted in the Silver camps. Quentin couldn't believe his good fortune. He was a chicken in a cornfield.

Quentin found his cabin at the end of a road off the main street. He had no neighbors yet; the surrounding places were shuttered.

Because he was so isolated, he was startled by a knock. His door opened, and a tall, muscular red-haired man entered. Quentin thought quickly and removed his shirt and trousers in preparation for an unplanned shower.

"Hey, uh, name's Murdough."

Quentin regarded the strapping lad over one shoulder. "Quentin."

"I'm the welcoming committee." He was blushing, stealing furtive glances at Quentin's derrière.

The shower water was lukewarm. He stepped in, soaping up, taking extra care to clean his hole, which had made so many men grunt and moan. He fingered his soapy ass, sliding in and out seductively. When he glanced over his shoulder, Murdough had built a tent in his trousers.

"You're welcome to join me."

Murdough closed and locked the front door. He stripped to his knickers. They cradled a massive set of balls and a hefty summer sausage-sized cock. He stepped into the shower still in his underwear. Quentin dropped the soap and rubbed his bare ass against the swelling mass between Murdough's legs while retrieving it.

Quentin lathered Murdough paying extra attention to the clothed areas.

"You don't need those now."

Murdough agreed. He shucked his underpants, revealing the full glory of his manhood. Freckled and plump, his penis grew thicker, stretching skyward from the patch of red pubic hair at the base of his shaft.

Quentin turned off the shower, knelt, and put him into his mouth. Murdough closed his eyes, no doubt picturing a girlfriend back home. Quentin coated Murdough's thick meat with saliva, the best lubricant available. He rose and put both hands against the shower wall, presenting his anus to the physically fit young man. Murdough was new, but instinct told him what to do. He was clumsy, but he found the entrance. He penetrated Quentin with inexperience. Although he was quite thick, he was an average length. He would not be visiting Quentin's interior room. Once inside, Murdough's animal-rutting instincts took over. He was young; his efforts were quick and effective. Within moments, he blew liquid pearls inside Quentin.

Quentin was glad to be of service to this handsome freckle-faced laborer. Murdough stayed hard. Twice more, he rutted to orgasm before he finally grew soft enough for Quentin to push him out. A soft dick and three loads of young come exited his stretched anus.

Sitting in the living room later, Quentin manipulated the young man for his selfish ends. First, he complimented the averagely endowed man. "You must be the biggest one in the camp!"

"No, Dale Clark is three times my size. He's the biggest."

"But you're surely next."

"No, there's Oswald Betancourt, Frank Simpson...those are the three I know for sure are huge."

Quentin pulled a second trick on the young man. "Please don't tell those men about me. You were more than I could handle."

"Oh, I won't."

Quentin watched the young man's eyes dart to the right, a sign he was lying. He would brag to them, as certain as Sunday.

"Thank you for your discretion, Murdough. I hope we can do this again soon."

"Welcome to Culebra Cut, Quentin. Do you know where everything is?"

"I think so. The mess hall is on Main Street. I passed it on the way in, right"?

"Yep. And you can catch a bus to work every morning right where they left you off."

"Mr. Murdough, you have made me feel exceptionally welcome here."

"We aim to please."

❦ 8 ❦

BIG, BIGGER, BIGGEST

No sooner had Quentin unpacked his possessions than there came another bold knock.

It was three Americans, precisely as he had expected. Men always brag, and they always lie.

"Gentlemen, welcome. Let me guess...Oswald, Frank and Dale."

"Right, but I'm Frank; he's Dale. How did you know"? Frank was short and stocky, with a black spray of chest hair escaping his open shirt collar.

"Frank, your reputation precedes you. They spoke about you in the brothels of Colón. All three of you have earned certain fame in these parts."

Oswald spoke, "You too. We hear you like it up the bum."

"You heard right. Now which of you is first? Frank"?

Frank Simpson needed no further encouragement. He undid his belt and let his trousers fall, revealing a long, fat, pink penis. He tugged ferociously at Quentin's pants until the button ripped, and they fell, revealing his small penis and his beautiful round buttocks.

This time, Quentin was prepared. He produced a tub of Vaseline, rubbing it liberally on and in his anus. Frank's penis grew longer and harder until it stood out at a 45-degree angle from his waist. Quentin bent over and spread his cheeks, inviting Frank inside.

The two men watched as Quentin expertly accepted Frank into his anal cavity. Frank moaned softly, then yelped when he felt his cock turn a corner he never knew existed. For the first time, he was buried completely inside a man.

"You fit so easily, Frank. I don't know why I struggled so with Murdough." He was playing mind games. Each man considered himself to be huge. Hearing that an average lad like Murdough was painful made them uneasy. Frank needed to prove his worth. He slammed in and out of Quentin feverishly, trying to get him to admit to pain. With Vaseline, pain was not likely. Plus, he still had slippery remnants of Murdough inside him.

Frank needed to hear he was bigger, better than the handsome Murdough. Quentin wanted only to please Frank now that he got him fucking at a frantic pace. He moaned.

"Oh, it hurts! Frank, you're hurting me!" Frank smiled and pounded harder, increasing the frequency with which he entered and exited Quentin's inner hole. Quentin's soft penis released a long string of clear semen. The two men watching remarked on it.

"Frank, you made him come like a girl."

That was all Frank needed to hear. His wounded pride was restored. He was victorious over his new conquest. With that, he released a hot spray of semen and pulled out violently. He sprayed more come onto Quentin's back and over his legs.

The two onlookers cheered. Frank excused himself for a shower. Oswald Betancourt stepped forward.

"You next, Ozzie"?

He was a bookish man. He was average in every way: average height, average intelligence, and average weight. Until he unbuttoned his linen trousers, revealing a colossal soft white cock.

"I need you to get me started." He held his jumbo penis like a flesh ice cream cone. Quentin leaned forward and gobbled the soft meat, swallowing it like a vitamin pill. Ozzie gasped. He never felt someone swallow him like a cannibal. His cock grew quickly, stretching Quentin's mouth and throat. Quentin continued to swallow the man, tasting salty fluid signaling his extreme pleasure and warning of an early release. For a moment, Quentin feared Oswald would come in his mouth - an awful waste. His fears were unfounded.

Oswald pulled out. He pushed Quentin onto the bed face up. He was going to fuck him missionary-style. The properness of the position matched his average appearance. But Oz was way beyond average in skill and size. He pushed his way into Quentin effortlessly, despite wielding a cock longer than a po' boy and bigger around than a can of baked beans. It was Quentin's turn to gasp as Oz pushed his way into the second chamber like it was his own bedroom. The girth of his erect penis stretched the doorway painfully. Quentin grabbed his sheets and sucked air through his teeth. Oz smiled sadistically. As more petroleum jelly worked its way inside, the stretching became pleasurable. Quentin moaned as he submitted to Oz's masterful fucking. Quentin could only enjoy the fucking because he knew his gasps and moans made Oz want to come.

"Oh, Oz, you're making me come." And again, a long trickle of clear fluid escaped my soft cock. Without warning, Oz grabbed his hips and plunged into him as deep as any man could. He held still, face red, and then released a loud breath.

"I'm coming"! And he filled Quentin with his syrupy semen.

Frank stood in a towel, watching the performance. He chuckled, and Oswald joined in. There was an inside joke, and Quentin wanted in.

"Sorry for the rude laughter, Q. It's just that we're worried for you."

"How do you mean"?

Frank answered. "If I am an orange, Oz is a grapefruit, wouldn't you say"?

He nodded.

"Dale is a watermelon." They both burst out laughing. Dale turned beet red.

"I can take him." Quentin boasted.

"You'd be the first. The doctor says he can't even have kids."

Dale growled at the men, "I don't want any goddamned children!"

Quentin sized up Dale. He was tall and robust, with black hair and blue eyes. His skin was the pale color of alabaster. His crotch seemed quite normal under his jeans.

Dale spoke. "Quentin, you're a nice guy. I can't do this. C'mon guys, let's go."

Quentin could not let this fish get away. "What excites you, Dale"?

"What do you mean"?

"What do you think about when you're pleasuring yourself"?

"Cunts. Asses. Little dicks."

"You already know I have a little dick. But did you know I have a cunt deep inside my ass"?

Frank added, "He does! I never fucked anything like it!"

Oz nodded.

Dale sighed. "I'm sure I could reach it if I could fit."

Frank praised Dale's endowment. "It's beyond massive. I don't think a cow could take him."

Dale smacked Frank.

"I'll show you, Quentin. But I don't expect you to follow through."

Dale lowered his jeans and extracted a soft wrinkled willy not much larger than Quentin's.

"Just give it a minute. Tell me about your cunt."

"Well, Dale, I only just discovered it myself on the steamship to Colón. A Spaniard with an extra long one turned a corner and popped right through. It makes me come like a girl."

"I see you come like a girl. Do you want me to make you come"?

Quentin glanced and drew a sharp breath. His cunt talk had aroused Dale. Quentin stared. Like a pneumatic tire, Dale's small soft endowment was inflating rapidly. What had been a very wrinkled piece of meat was extending and thickening into a colossus. The cock kept growing far beyond anything Quentin had ever seen. It was a log of liverwurst between his legs. It was perfectly smooth.

Dale folded his arms defiantly. "See"?

Quentin's need to please clashed violently with his self-preservation instinct. He seriously could die pleasing this monster. His male-centered gratification won out. If he must die in the effort, so be it.

Dale bent to pull his pants.

"What are you doing"?

Dale smirked. "What? You think you'll be the first to take me on? I haven't been inside anyone, ever."

Quentin hefted the six-pound hunk of meat and liberally applied Vaseline. He added a tablespoon to his insides.

Dale lay back on the bed. His towering cock glistened with jelly. Quentin straddled the edifice and placed his butt on top. He needed help.

"Dale, can you fit a finger inside me?"

He could. Then two, then three.

"Stretch me, Dale."

In a few minutes, Dale was past the knuckles. Quentin's hole encircled his wrist.

"Keep going."

Dale's arm went deep.

"Now make a fist and try to pull it out."

Dale pulled and twisted his fist until it finally came out with a loud pop. Quentin suppressed a scream.

"Put it back in."

Dale repeated the motion several times until his full fist could punch its way in quickly. Quentin hid the tears from him.

"Now we're ready, Dale." He placed his butt at the top of the tower again. This time, he was able to let Dale penetrate him. Every inch was agony, but Quentin was determined to please his man.

Dale's eyes widened. He had never felt this before. It was much better than he had hoped. Quentin smiled and let gravity impale him further on the gargantuan penis. Progress was agonizingly slow. The smile across Dale's face spread pleasure to mingle with the dolorous spasms in his rectum.

Two painful minutes later, Quentin felt Dale reach the rear wall. He had no idea if he could go any further. Like Massimo, Dale was rock hard and impossibly thick. He checked; Dale still had three inches to go. Quentin contemplated riding Dale without full penetration. It was his first time inside a person. He wouldn't know if he was missing something. But Quentin was a perfectionist. He wouldn't feel true pleasure until he allowed Dale to enter him completely.

Oz and Frank stood slack-jawed. Never in their lives had they witnessed such bravery. Quentin's flat belly bulged with the mass of flesh he pushed inside himself.

Dale wept softly with gratitude and joy. He was losing his virginity at last. No woman would ever have him. He had been ejected from every brothel. But this kind, patient man was willing to sacrifice himself on the dick of death. But then something remarkable happened. Quentin leaned and bore down hard until Dale entered the inner passage beyond the anal canal.

Quentin wanted to scream. Never had he endured such pain in his life. The fist-sized head of Dale's cock punched past the doorway, stretching and tearing him internally. He needed to see Dale enjoying this, or he wouldn't make it. Dale was in ecstasy. Sex had been forbidden him. He was learning the joys of copulation from an expert.

"Q, you feel so good."

That was the words he needed. He lifted himself, withdrawing Dale from the inner room, then sat hard, taking him fully. The inner doorway stretched but didn't tear. It felt so good to be filled far beyond capacity. Dale's cock was as big as a newborn baby. Quentin closed his eyes and gave birth over and over, riding him at an ever-increasing pace.

Dale's moans caused Quentin to leak the clear fluid from his tiny soft penis. He raised and lowered his butt to the rhythm of Dale's heavy breaths. They grew shallower, increasing the speed. Dale bit his lower lip and whined. He had painstakingly brought himself to orgasm before, but this was far more powerful. Each time he entered the inner chamber, his cockhead throbbed. He could feel his own clear fluid seeping out.

Dale's hips began to thrust of their own accord. Quentin had waited for this moment. He rotated position and commanded Dale to stand.

"It will feel best if you do the fucking."

Dale nodded. He grabbed hold of Quentin's hips and thrust in and out. It was an animal instinct, the need for the male to pound his hips into his partner. With Dale in control, the satisfaction of pleasing him completely eclipsed any pain. Quentin was leaking like a faucet, making a map of France on his clean linens. Dale's strokes grew longer and more violent. Quentin was in a mystical state where pleasure and agony intertwined to form a hybrid sensation, which lifted his spirit out of his body. No man had ever violated him so completely. Dale was the thickest and the longest he had ever taken.

Frank and Oz were dumbstruck. What they saw seemed physically impossible. Dale's massive cock forced its way deep into the man. Quentin touched his belly and felt the grotesque organ push to the surface with each inward thrust. It was how he imagined a baby kicking would feel. The birth and baby theme was new for him. Pretending he was pregnant, giving birth over and over again, caused him to grow hard. He didn't want Dale to see, in case it disgusted him.

Dale was approaching climax. He fucked with reckless abandon. Nothing could touch him now. He was soaring high above the clouds.

Quentin felt Dale grow impossibly large inside him. He knew what was coming. The pressure of the added girth caused the boy's hard cock to throb. Clear fluid no longer flowed. Without touching himself, Quentin was going to ejaculate fully.

Dale's groans dissolved into grunts. Like a pig, he slammed his oversized cock far inside Quentin. He cried out and released.

Just as a baby's cry made a mother's milk flow, so too did Dale's cry send Quentin over the edge, shooting volumes of milky white semen across his bed. Inside, he felt the hot flood of Dale's sperm. The man behind him was shuddering, his legs trembling. He stayed buried inside Quentin for several minutes, fully erect. There was a smattering of applause from the audience.

Frank whispered to Oz, who nodded.

Dale began to shrink, bringing relief to Quentin's battered and stretched hole. He expelled the cock on a river of semen. This time there was blood.

Frank spoke. "Q, you gave a powerful performance,

unlike anything we've seen. Oz and me, we got to thinking. Could you take us both at once"?

Quentin felt every nerve in his lower digestive tract
throbbing with pain. He saw the hunger in the men's
eyes. He was stretched, bruised, and torn, so what
worse could they do? He nodded.

Frank lay on the bed, stiff as a board with excitement. Quentin lowered himself easily onto Frank, who
seemed so small to him now. Frank went past the
second door with scarcely a wince from Quentin.

Quentin laid back against Frank's chest and raised
his legs. This provided a front entrance for Oswald. Oz
pressed his meat against Frank's, allowing him to penetrate Quentin. Together, the two well-hung men were
hard to accommodate. Although they were not solid
like Dale, they stretched Quentin in new and painful
ways. Soon, the two men were both fully inside.

As they each fucked Quentin to their own rhythm,
he felt a cacophonous symphony of movements inside.
With time, the two men realized how good it felt to
coordinate their movements. In truth, they were giving
one another pleasure, and Quentin was merely the receptacle to hold their huge cocks and permit them to
slide against one another.

This was a new role for Quentin. He was facilitating
pleasure between two friends buried deep inside him. It
caused him to have his womanly orgasm. He leaked
from his tiny soft cock, which had withdrawn inside
him in reaction to the pain of two cocks. It resembled a
large clitoris.

Oswald was teaching Frank how to fuck. Frank was
a quick study. Soon both men were pleasuring Quentin
and one another in steady strokes, perfectly timed.
Frank pulled Oz to his lips. They explored one another's mouths. Quentin was in a state of bliss. He watched
love blossom between two men whom he held tightly
inside him. The flow of love from one through him to

the other was so exciting that Quentin experienced multiple female-like orgasms. His little clitoris seeped clear cum in wave after wave. The waves caused him to contract, squeezing the two newfound lovers more tightly. It was too much; they couldn't hold back. Their kisses became hungry and rough.

Oz touched one of Frank's nipples, and he bucked. Oz tickled it lightly until Frank moaned. He switched nipples.

"Oh shit! I'm gonna come!" And in seconds, Ropes of hot semen filled Quentin and basted both men's cocks. The added slipperiness caused Oswald to teeter over the precipice. A new flood filled the anal cavity.

The two men were so deeply engaged in kissing that they scarcely noticed when peristalsis forced their soft cocks from Quentin's sperm-soaked aching hole.

9

THROAT EXAM

After breakfast and a short bus ride, Quentin limped to the field accounting office early. The internal bruising and torn openings made every step a challenge. There he met his many coworkers. Most were childless women whose husbands were architects or civil engineers. They kept busy adding rows and columns of numbers and then double-entering them into the General ledger and the current accounts. Quentin knew accounting well. He was a great addition to this busy office.

Quentin had trouble remaining seated. The women watched as the color slowly drained from his face. The women had all suffered waterborne illnesses, which bore a passing resemblance to Quentin's state of health. They sent for the doctor, suspecting amoebic dysentery. He tried to fight off the medical staff, insisting he was fine. They took him to the field hospital. Here, jaundiced victims of fever and malaria lay in beds fighting for their lives. Quentin knew precisely what had caused the problem, and its initials were DHC: Dale's Huge Cock.

What Quentin didn't know was that he had been ruptured and lacerated in several places. He was slowly losing blood. By the time they reached the hospital,

Quentin was too weak to stand. They wheeled him to an examination table, where he lost consciousness.

He awoke to a sunny bed. His insides still ached, but a euphoric feeling akin to a waking dream dulled the pain. He knew it must be morphine. In the hallways, the nurses spoke at low volume. Quentin could not decipher the whispers but recognized their judgmental frowns. They were the faces of the family he left in New Orleans.

A doctor entered the room, locking the door. He was handsome, with gleaming white teeth, sky-blue eyes, and a constant blush Quentin found endearing. "Good morning, Mr. Fournier; I'm Dr. Heimert."

He consulted a chart. "You were admitted for symptoms of amoebic dysentery. But we can both safely conclude dysentery is not your diagnosis."

Now it was Quentin's turn to blush.

"I told them I knew the cause."

"Who attacked you"?

"Attacked? I had a party in my room last night. Nobody attacked anyone."

Heimert tilted his head and gave a smile Quentin knew and loved. They were part of the same secret family. "So, you incurred these injuries through your own choice"?

"I'll do it again as soon as I am able."

"We examined your throat and gave it a clean bill of health." As the doctor said this, he discreetly adjusted the crotch of his pants. A bulge protruded.

Quentin smiled and leaned back, allowing his head to loll over the side of the hospital bed. From this angle, the doctor would have a smooth ride to the back of Quentin's throat.

The doctor unzipped and presented a long, thin cock. He inserted it ¾ of the way where he hit the tonsil blockade. He was surprised Quentin did not gag. He was ten times as surprised when Quentin swallowed

Heimert's cock deep down his esophagus. The doctor was paralyzed, unsure if he should move deeper and risk suffocating his patient. Quentin lifted his head and dropped it, letting the cock go as far inside as possible, then letting it slip past the epiglottis, creating a stroking sensation most men never experience. Dr. Heimert was among the blessed few to know the pleasures of full-throat fucking. Quentin held the doctor's round buttocks and encouraged him to start bucking and thrusting. If his mouth weren't so full, he would have said, "Don't hold back." He pulled the doctor forward and back until, at last, he understood Quentin's mouth belonged to him now. He could extract satisfaction from his gaping maw with no reticence.

The doctor was overcome with the animal lusts that drive men to rut. His hips rocked violently back and forth. His long cock ran across the epiglottis, where all cocks should go but rarely do. This flap of cartilage, which prevents food from entering the windpipe, is also a highly erotic narrow spot in the throat. It gives the illusion that someone is running a finger up and down the end of your cock. Short cocks can't reach it. Quentin was anatomically deprived and would never know how much pleasure he was giving the doctor at this very moment.

But Quentin was different from most men. He didn't need his cock sucked to feel pleasure. He just needed to ensure he was pleasing another man.

He had total assurance from the doctor, who was getting a surprise anatomy lesson from his patient. Never had his wife been able to perform such feats. She disliked oral sex, putting Heimert's cock in her vagina as quickly as possible. This led to an unfortunately large litter of children. If she let him in her mouth or ass, they could keep the baby-making at bay. Now he knew a gold bachelor with many talents. He may not need his wife at all now.

The doctor was puzzled by the damage to Quentin's interior. He clearly engaged in anal sex, as evidenced by the many puddles of semen inside. But he wondered why he was hurt so badly.

The doctor set these thoughts aside and concentrated on bringing himself to climax. He could get close if he stayed buried deep for a minute or more. He knew this would deprive his patient of oxygen. He needed two full minutes ramming past the epiglottis to reach orgasm. He withdrew his cock entirely, letting threads of saliva drip to the floor and forehead.

"Can you hold your breath a long time"?

Quentin nodded. He opened his mouth and reached for the Doctor's extra-long cock like a baby bird stretching to pluck a worm from its mother's mouth. He inhaled a large breath of air, then the man's entire length. The doctor went deep, taking short strokes, ensuring his patient's epiglottis would scrape hard against the end of his cock.

Quentin didn't panic. He disliked holding his breath for so long. He felt an increasing urge to regurgitate his breakfast. But these feelings weren't important. His job was to please his doctor and let him use his throat like a vagina. The doctor picked up his pace, blowing out short bursts. Sweat formed in droplets on his forehead, splashing. Just as Quentin became convinced he would pass out from lack of oxygen, he saw Heimert's balls contract. The doctor threw his head back. "Yes! Take it!" Deep inside his patient's throat, he expelled bursts of semen repeatedly. Quentin felt it squirt inside him twice before he pulled his head away with a hoarse cough allowing air to fill his lungs. The doctor's long cock continued to shoot, splashing his tonsils, then his tongue, and as it left his mouth, the meat stick sprayed more come on Quentin's face. Then, as if nothing had happened, he consulted the chart.

"I'm going to give you laudanum for the pain. You

need to limit your motion to keep your wounds from reopening. You swallowed several ounces of my semen. It should be fine."

"May I go back to work"?

"I'll write a letter asking you to return in three days. You need to stay in bed to allow the torn flesh in your rectum and sigmoid colon to heal."

Quentin nodded. Then he grew curious. "Will there be scars"?

"Yes, I'm afraid so, although they won't be visible."

"So am I going to tear again easily"?

The doctor put a pencil to his upper lip. "No. The scar tissue will be much thicker."

Quentin got dressed while the doctor watched.

"As a doctor, I would like to ask what happened to cause so much damage."

Quentin didn't hesitate. "Frank Simpson fucked me, as did Oswald Betancourt. Dale Clark took some doing, but I got him in. Then both Oswald and Frank did me at once."

The pencil hit the floor. The doctor didn't bother retrieving it.

"I know all three of those men. Dale Clark is incapable of penetration. He's come to me asking for help, which I cannot give. Nature's blessing is a curse for that man."

"I was his first."

The doctor shook his head. "You are talented, but please be careful your talents don't kill you, son."

Quentin gave the same nod one might see an alcoholic give when promising to swear off the drink.

10

A NIGHT TO REGRET

After three days of laudanum and bed rest, Quentin was ready for a new adventure. Dale had been to see him twice. He brought flowers the second time. Quentin knew he must learn to take Dale, for he was the man's only hope of having any kind of sex life. But Dale understood he needed to wait. He had gone his whole life waiting. A few more weeks were tolerable.

Quentin knew that it would be hard to enjoy other men once he allowed Dale in again. His loose, stretched hole would not satisfy other men. Quentin had searched many hundreds of men to please, and none had found greater pleasure than Dale. He was the one who would snare Quentin for good. Quentin would allow his anatomy to become permanently altered by Dale's battering ram. The flowers said all this. Dale would never find satisfaction without him.

Before Quentin committed to this one needy man, he wanted to feel a burning need from others.

On the third night of his recovery, Quentin felt ready to get back on the horse, so to speak. He took a tub of Vaseline and a flashlight. He followed the trail down to the silver camps. The men were segregated by ethnicity. One cabin housed Caribbean and American black men. Another held Spaniards and Caribbean Spanish speakers; the third was Italian.

Quentin saw Massimo, the Roman whom he had once thought the biggest, thickest man he would ever take. He seemed almost normal to him now.

Massimo asked if he wanted to give him his ass, and Quentin obliged. Massimo took him to the telegraph office, which was closed for the night.

Quentin bent over the desk and lowered his buttocks enough to allow the short man easy entry.

This time, Quentin finally gave Massimo the surprise he had held back. His anatomy had already been changed by a single night with Dale. Massimo slipped into the inner chamber. When Massimo's hips came in contact with Quentin's buttocks, he gasped.

"Did I put the hole in you"?

Quentin smiled and shook his head. "I saved this for you as a surprise."

Massimo rutted fiercely, groaning before he released his semen in the inner room.

Quentin felt none of the pain or discomfort he had felt earlier with Massimo. It was good, but he longed for more. Massimo buckled his belt.

"Before you go, can I ask a favor"?

"Si, yes."

"Will you let the other men know I am in here"?

Massimo nodded and left.

Quentin waited eagerly. He heard the door open, but with the lights off, he couldn't see who had entered.

It was someone new, a black man. The man was enormous like Carlo, but nothing like Dale. His thrusts were hurried and desperate. Quentin felt very full but still experienced no pain. The man was familiar with the inner room and quickly found his way there. Quentin felt the man's pleasure increase. He imbibed the man's delight and increased his own. It was not long before he reached climax. Quentin took the man's sperm and released him back into the night.

A line of strangers formed. One by one, Quentin invited them to use him as a receptacle to spill their cum. He took men of all shapes, sizes, and colors. With each new man, Quentin's rectum filled with fluid. He expelled it periodically so a sticky puddle formed at his feet. The puddle grew. With one enormous Columbian, he himself grew hard and added his own white semen to the gooey mess below.

Quentin had never allowed himself to be a whore to so many men in one night. He loved facing away from them, so he only came to know them by their hands, their technique, and the shape of their cock inside him. No one wanted conversation. They were here for a gratifying release. It was many hours before the line grew shorter. The messy puddle of semen had become a hazard. One man had slipped, stabbing Quentin in the gut. It felt like a feather compared to Dale.

Men returned with towels and used their feet to mop around Quentin and whoever was inside him at that moment. Quentin felt some younger men enter him a second time. He knew their skin, their thrusts, and their cocks. As he filled with semen, a paradoxically empty feeling troubled him. He thought that with each new satisfied cock he would feel his happiness increase, which it did initially. But now, six hours later, he was weary of the excess. He expelled another measure of semen. As it left him, he felt something new. He felt lonely. He couldn't claim to be alone with so many men pleasuring themselves inside him. And yet this was how he felt.

Indeed, when the last man had found pleasure inside him and deposited his semen, Quentin was left alone to clean the floor. He cried for the first time since infancy.

It was near dawn. In two hours, he would need to report to work.

During the walk uphill, he soiled his dungarees. Several ounces of semen left in his sigmoid colon had found their way out of his loose anus. He cursed himself and his greed for satisfying men.

When he reached his cabin, he studied the doctor's note. He didn't return until the next day so that he could rest after all.

He threw his dirty trousers into the hamper and showered, scrubbing himself inside and out. He tried to wash away the shame, but it was useless. He looked at his below-average penis and felt an inner rage at God for making him this way. He could never satisfy anyone the way these men satisfied him. He was designed by nature to be a whore for men to use. He longed to feel their pleasure, but he needed to feel their gratitude. Last night had taught him this. None of these strangers thanked him for his service. They simply used them, exchanged pleasure with him during the buildup to orgasm, then walked away.

Quentin remembered Carlo, the Sicilian, who kissed him with gratitude for curing him of his fainting spells. He thought about Oz and Frank, two men with huge cocks who discovered a love for one another sharing his hole.

Quentin glanced at the vase of tropical flowers Dale had brought him. Gratitude. Far more intoxicating than mere pleasure.

He drifted into a dreamless sleep.

❧ 11 ❧

DALE FINDS HIS FIT

Quentin awoke at noon. Dale sat by his bed. He looked longingly at Quentin. He had a tongue sandwich for Quentin, who quickly realized he was famished. They spoke very little. Dale put his big hand on Quentin's forehead. No fever.

"Quentin, can I get you anything"?

"I need you to hold me."

Dale brightened at the request. He climbed under the sheet and wrapped his big arm around Quentin. Quentin could feel a swelling in Dale's groin. It grew rapidly and stretched Dale's pants so hard a seam ripped.

"I'm so sorry. Being near you like this..."

Quentin turned and put a finger to Dale's lips. Then he kissed him. Dale kissed back. They were following a dangerous path. Quentin. Put his hand on Dale's leg near where the head of his penis was trapped. He traced circle eights across its mass, causing Dale to shudder.

Quentin didn't want to return to the hospital, but failing to gratify this huge handsome man was worse than any physical pain he had endured.

"Dale, I'm ready for you."

"But...are you sure"?

Quentin nodded. He undid Dale's belt. After some struggle, Dale's gargantuan penis escaped his trousers. Freed from its prison, it flew skywards, then fell with gravity, landing on Quentin's abdomen and chest. Free from tight pants, it spread longer and wider.

Quentin shuddered, fear mingling with intense desire. He spread Vaseline along its length, repeating several times until every inch of skin was coated and glistening.

Dale applied jelly around and inside the anus. He used his hands to gently stretch Quentin wider. Then, with more force, he steadily applied pressure until his hand was engulfed. He formed a fist, just as Quentin had taught him, and tried removing it. To his surprise, it came out easy. Quentin blinked. He felt no pain. The laudanum had long since left his system; it defied explanation.

Dale inserted his clenched fist inside again. He observed Quentin's face carefully, but all he saw were fluttering eyes.

"Am I hurting you"?

"You should be, but you're not. I don't know why."

"Shall I keep going"?

In answer, Quentin pulled the fist from inside him and pushed it back inside in a smooth motion. Once both were convinced Quentin was prepared, Dale positioned his head at the puckered entryway to pleasure and desire. He pressed in easily.

Quentin grabbed Dale by his shirt and kissed him deeply. He felt his small penis harden with desire. He wanted Dale. He didn't just want Dale to feel pleasure like before. He wanted Dale to make love to him. He wanted to be filled with Dale Clark.

As these new desires flooded Quentin's heart and

brain, Dale's destroyer slipped right in, hitting the rectum wall with a soft landing.

"Q, you don't have to try to take more of me."

Quentin felt between his legs. The length of Dale's exposed cock was too many inches. It was obscene to leave so much meat exposed to the wind.

Contorting his abdomen, Quentin found the scarred passageway to accept Dale completely. In a smooth motion, Dale's cockhead pushed four inches into the colon. Dale's hips were pressed lightly against the buttocks. Quentin grasped Dale's muscular buttocks and pressed his hips tightly until his cockhead was five inches past the inner door.

Dale closed his eyes. He felt like he could stay there forever, deep inside this man who had nearly died to join with him. Dale loved him. It was so simple. He loved him. He wanted to make love to him.

Quentin, forever tuned to subtle energies, felt Dale's sudden awakening hit him like a mule kicking him in the head. With every inch buried deep inside him, this silent telegraph signal of love swirled between them. Dale had not moved, pressed further inside his newfound love than any other man could.

Dale withdrew eight inches before smoothly sliding back in completely. His balls spanked Quentin's beautiful round buttocks. As Dale thrust back and forth, his lover entered an altered consciousness. He was intensely in his body, but his brain flew him to a meadow. In the field, Dale lay on his back, his gigantic cock growing longer and thicker. From high above, Quentin fell earthward. Dale's cock caught his fall and entered him, stretching him and filling him with its immensity. Quentin returned to his bed with a loud gasp as one of Dale's thrusts missed the inner door and pummeled his rectum. It was painful, sensual, and delightful.

"Oh Q, Sorry--"

Quentin silenced his man with a deep tongue kiss. It

was the first kiss since each had realized they loved the other. Combined with the mutual joy of penetrating and being penetrated, the kiss multiplied their erotic pleasure.

Dale found a sweet spot where the length of his strokes was just right to tickle Quentin's inner door and squeeze his own cockhead. To accomplish this, he had to press his belly against Quentin's. Dale's belly rubbed continually against Quentin's hard penis, making it drool.

The inner tickling sent Quentin to a new place he never even dreamed he belonged. While Dale marveled he could insert his penis inside anyone, let alone this man he loved, Quentin groaned from the intensity of having his inner door thrown wide open and slammed shut every two seconds. It caused a fireball to form in his belly and travel to his crotch. With Dale's belly stimulating him, Quentin realized he was about to come.

The fireball was felt by both, for Dale's cock head had been pressed and released hundreds of times now, and his balls were burning with a fresh delivery of seed.

Quentin said, "Dale, you're making me come." He kissed Dale hard as the first rope of jism exploded from his tiny cock and hit Dale under the chin.

"Oh shit!" Dale released his first shot of cum while buried completely in his man.

Quentin had never allowed himself to enjoy orgasm like a man. He shot load after load of semen, landing on the furniture, in Dale's hair, up his own nose. He grunted and squeezed out the final drops, tasting them. His semen was sweet and syrupy, unlike the salty clear fluid he leaked like a girl.

Dale was pulling back rapidly. The second shot hit the back of the rectum. His third shot filled Quentin's anal canal with a saucerful of hot seed. His next squirt was outside. It landed on Quentin's lips. He opened his mouth to catch the next, then licked his lips.

Dale thought he would never stop. He landed another shot in Quentin's mouth, then shot into his own mouth. Quentin kissed him, the semen intermingling in their mouths.

Dale's cock was still rock hard. He had another go in him but wanted to give Quentin a break.

Quentin pushed Dale back on the bed and impaled himself on the towering cock. With great skill, he rocked his behind back and forth until he was sitting on Dale's lap. With gravity's assistance, he pressed downward until he could feel Dale's pubic bone between his butt cheeks.

Quentin was a natural acrobat. He used his legs to propel himself upward, then let gravity bring him back down. He repeated this motion for several minutes. Dale lay on his back and watched his love perform his feats of endurance and bravery. On one upward movement, Quentin overshot, and Dale's cock came out.

Dale couldn't believe what he saw. Quentin's rectum was so stretched it remained open. He could see into the hole. Then Quentin slid right back down without using his hands. He wanted to see it again, so he lifted the man off of his cock each time, then watched in astonishment as the gaping hole found its target every time, burying Dale to the hilt.

The gaping hairless hole bookmarked by two perfect round buttocks was too much for Dale. He had no time to warn Q. As he came springing skyward, his gaping anus hovered over Dale's cock head. Out of the slit came a massive load of white spew. Like a sharpshooter, Dale fired it right into Quentin's wide-open hole. He repeated a masterful series of shots several times until his last drops merely cascaded down the outside of his towering elephant's trunk of a penis.

Quentin felt each load land inside him without

touching his hole. He could feel a breeze blowing and wondered how much Dale had stretched him. After the last load landed inside his gaping hole, he stood and let the semen from both rounds start to pour. Like icing on a cake, they landed all over the massive cock of the man he now loved. He turned and licked the icing from his man's cake.

EPILOGUE - A LID FOR
EVERY POT

Quentin had journeyed to Panama in search of endless encounters with men. He found love instead. Dale had escaped to Panama to forget his 'curse' only to have it transformed into a blessing when he met the one person on Earth who could take him. The fact it was a man who could accommodate him meant very little, for this man was extraordinary in every way. Better still, they fell in love with one another. There was a lid for every pot.

After two deadly outbreaks of yellow fever, the loving couple chose to leave the tropics for safer climes. They took their hard-earned gold and moved to San Francisco.

Quentin never again felt pain with Dale. The love they shared and the constant lovemaking left them perfectly in tune with one another. Quentin acclimated but never grew tired of taking one of the world's most enormous cocks deep inside him. They found hundreds of new ways to please one another. Dale's favorite trick was to end lovemaking with Quentin lying face down on the bed, remove his cock and play target practice with the gaping hole he had made. Quentin jumped with surprise as each ball of come found its mark.

Quentin found sex with Dale so stimulating that he

could no longer ignore his own cock. The soft dribbling female orgasms of his youth were replaced with confident, manly ejaculations. Despite his small dick, he had a very long range. His favorite ending was to shoot into Dale's open mouth while sitting on his hard cock. Because he had so little to aim with, his spigot was less precise than Dale's garden hose. But he always managed to soak Dale's face from below.

Quentin was heartbroken to learn his beloved spinster Aunt Lisette passed away. He was astonished to learn she truly loved and accepted him. She left her entire fortune to him with a will so solid no lawyer from his family could contest it. Dale and Quentin were suddenly very rich.

Years later, Dale and Quentin ran into Oswald and Frank at the Olympic Club. They convinced Dale to let them celebrate their first union by recreating that night with Quentin. Quentin took the couple effortlessly. He let them slide and pound their way into him, rubbing against each other's penises until they painted his insides white. Then Dale used their come to lubricate his masterful lovemaking. It was a repeat performance with a very happy ending.

The End

Did you like this novel? Please LEAVE A REVIEW

ABOUT THE AUTHORS

Peter Schutes is the nom de plume of a prolific and acclaimed novelist. As Peter Schutes, he is the author of Adult Erotic Fiction such as <u>The Slaves of Rome</u>, <u>Dark as a Dungeon</u>, <u>The Gospel of Priapus</u>, and <u>Panama Heat</u>. He writes in the style of vintage pulp authors from the 1960s and 1970s. He lives in Los Angeles.

Adam Maxwell Bigglesworth is the pen name of an aristocratic one-time heir to the throne of Scotland and a literary novelist. Adam is the author of many novellas and short stories, including Chopper Jock and Satan's Sissy Boy. Although his family lives in the Midlands of England, his roots are on the Isle of Lewis in the Outer Hebrides.

OTHER BOOKS FROM PETER SCHUTES PUBLISHING

E-books and Paperbacks

The Able Seaman

The Anaconda Copper

The Autobiography of Peter Schutes

Backwoods Delivery

Big Bodies of All Sizes

Big Hole River

Bunkhouse Buddies

The Butt Baby

Cloistered

Confessions of a Rodeo Clown

Dark as a Dungeon

Demonic Deception *aka* Deceived, Cursed & Blessed

Desert Island Daddies

Dirty Dorms and Fresh Men

The Expectant Member

Firehouse Lovers

The Fish

Five Erotic Tales

The Gospel of Priapus

Hercules and Lippos

Hobo Honey

Hot Blue Collars

Hotshot

Logger's Delight

Muscle Bottom

Panama Heat

Satanic Seductions

Satan's Sissy Boy

The Slaves of Rome

The Thigh Baby

Under the Boardwalk

World's Biggest

***** Coming Soon *****

Like the Greeks Do

Hoboes, Hustlers, and Jailbirds

Small Cockpits and Big Hangars

Tales of Two Daddies

More Tales of Two Daddies

9 781963 667080